Living
Arrangements

Living Arrangements

Laura Maylene Walter

Winner of the G.S. Sharat Chandra Prize for
Short Fiction selected by Robert Olen Butler

BkMk Press
University of Missouri-Kansas City

BkMk Press
University of Missouri-Kansas City
5101 Rockhill Road
Kansas City, Missouri 64110
(816) 235-2558 (voice)
(816) 235-2611 (fax)
www.umkc.edu/bkmk

**Missouri
Arts Council**
The State of the Arts

Financial assistance for this project has been provided by the
Missouri Arts Council, a state agency.

Cover Design: Amanda Tinoco
Book interior design: Susan L. Schurman
Author Photo: Peter Garver
Managing Editor: Ben Furnish
Editorial Assistant: Linda D. Brennaman
The G. S. Chandra Prize for Short Fiction wishes to thank
Naomi Benaron, Leslie Koffler, Linda Rodriguez, and Jane Wood.
BkMk Press also wishes to thank Nicholas Sawin, Megan Hardeman, Sarah Eyer,
Pamela Rasch, Christine Pivovar, Rachel Sweet, and Paul Tosh.

Library of Congress Cataloging-in-Publication Data

Walter, Laura Maylene.
Living arrangements / Laura Maylene Walter.
  p. cm.
"Winner of the G.S. Sharat Chandra Prize for Short Fiction selected by Robert Olen
Butler."
  ISBN 978-1-886157-80-4 (pbk.: alk. paper)
  I. Title.
PS3623.A44685 L58 2011
813'.6--dc23

                                                2011033439

This book is set in Garamond Premier Pro, Qlassik, Optima.

In memory of my mother

Acknowledgments

I wrote the stories in this collection between 2005 and 2009. During that time, I participated in various writing groups and met many writers along the way. While I cannot possibly thank every reader who had a part in helping me shape these stories, please know I am grateful for your insight and your influence on my writing.

Thank you to Huda Al-Marashi and Jennifer Marie Donahue for your support, camaraderie, and laughter over these last few years. You two are the best writing buddies anyone could ask for, and I know I'm a stronger writer because of you. Thanks also to John Frank for the encouragement and the laughs, Amy Mescia for keeping me sane, Anthony Lauder for the Czech help, and Charlie Oberndorf for the generous critiques and the writing group invitation—and thanks to everyone there for welcoming the new kid to your ranks. I'd also like to extend heartfelt thanks to Ben Furnish and the staff at BkMk Press for making my debut book publishing experience such a positive one.

Finally, I'd like to thank my husband, Peter Garver, for his unfailing patience and encouragement—even when I didn't allow him to read my writing for the better part of a decade.

Some of the stories in this collection previously appeared, in slightly different form, in the following journals:

"Living Arrangements" in the *American Literary Review*
"To Elizabeth Bishop, with Love," in *Inkwell*
"Live Model" in *Crab Creek Review*
"The Ballad Solemn of Lady Malena" in *South Dakota Review*
"How to Speak Czech" in *Mason's Road*
"The Second Rule of Yoga" in *The Northville Review*
"Return to Stillbrook Farm" in *Three Coyotes*

Living Arrangements

Foreword

The stories in *Living Arrangements* are rooted in the most important principles of literary art. They are not content simply to render the problems of characters; they transform those problems into the dynamic of desire, which drives all great narrative. And the desire in these stories is that of most great literature: the desire for self, the desire for a place in the world, in the universe. *Living Arrangements* is a splendid recipient of the redoubtable G. S. Sharat Chandra Prize for Short Fiction.

Robert Olen Butler
Final Judge, G. S. Sharat Chandra Prize for Short Fiction

Living Arrangements

Caterpillar House

The first house is in upstate New York, a brick ranch with a sickly linden tree and a chain-link run for the Old English sheepdog. Your parents shave the dog in hot weather and then complain when his hair grows in coarse and wiry. He weighs more than your mother. She lets him pull her around the neighborhood on his red leash while she waves and laughs to the neighbors. Her hair is blond. She is at her most beautiful during this time, but you wouldn't know it. You are a newborn, a wrinkled girl confined to your crib, the high chair, the stroller.

That summer, the house suffers a plague of caterpillars. Hundreds of them, green and fuzzy, wriggle their way up the bricks on the outside of the house. Your parents stand spraying the walls with water, knocking the caterpillars down. Some live, some drown. Neither of your parents realize that this is the summer to remember. This is a time your family is happy, your mother vibrant and young.

They pack up the moving vans in September, when you are nine months old. You sleep the entire drive to Pennsylvania, cozy and protected in the car seat, every bump on the roadway pounding like a heartbeat.

Porch of the Lions

The second house has modest architecture, a shiny black mailbox hanging on the white siding by the front door. You pretend to be a lion on the front stoop, conjure castles inside the lilac bush, and fashion fallen seedpods into imaginary fish. On hot days you shimmy under the porch in the cool dirt and touch the backs of pillbugs gently, gently, until they roll into themselves.

This backyard holds a pear tree, and there you find a plump mother bird feeding her babies in its branches. The pears fall and rot on the ground, attracting bugs, but you play there anyway, pushing your doll stroller across the crimped grass. You love much about this house: the screened-in porch, the multicolored shag carpeting, the crawl space under the stairs packed with old stuffed animals, the swivel chairs in the kitchen, the avocado refrigerator, the magnets painted to look like brown and orange daisies.

When you are four years old, you wake up in the middle of the night and sneak to the top of the stairs and peer down to see Santa putting gifts under the tree. Everything is shimmery and slightly out of focus, like a Christmas fog has drifted through the living room. Years later, you decide it must have been a dream, but you'll never quite convince yourself.

Every Christmas, your mother fills the house with stars. She beams and holds you in front of the Christmas tree. She sets out all the presents, the line of stockings with names written in glue and glitter. Pine needles and tinsel bits will riddle the carpet for months to come, reminders that your mother worked to give you magic.

Construction Site

Your father's business takes off, and the family gets what it has not known before: money. They make plans to leave the white house with the picture window and the pear tree and the crawl space under the stairs. First come long drives to the edge of neighborhoods to look at bare plots of land, and then the maps appear, great blue ones with skinny crisscrossing lines. The house will be new from the bottom up, from the inside out, your mother tells you. It will belong entirely to the family.

Whole crowds of trees must fall to make way for your house. You don't know it, but this infuriates the neighbors. Your family visits the construction site many times. It smells like dirt and then lumber and then paint. In the winter, you make a miniature snowman to hold in your hand, and fly into a temper when his head falls off and smashes against the ground.

Your parents drag you with them when they go shopping. There is so much to buy, so much that goes into a house that you never considered. Hardwood flooring, carpet, linoleum, windows, screens, drapes, blinds, furniture, art, frames, knickknacks. The shopping excursions are the low point of your six years. You wrap yourself in the display curtains and touch all the carpet samples, but still you get bored. Some stores have a corner sectioned off for toys; these are the best ones. Others leave you with nothing but a round rack full of customers' coats. You crawl into the center and find this moment of dark, of being hidden, better than anything in the toy chest.

At least you get to decorate your own room. You choose pale purple paint, a unicorn bedspread, and matching curtains. Your mother helps you pick everything out, and when the house is ready she puts it all together for you. Try to remember this. She will never help you move again.

Mansion on the Hill

The new house is a big four-bedroom Colonial with cedar siding. It stands by itself on the top of a steep hill in front of the rest of the woods that weren't chopped down. The body of the house is imposing, the tall, flat windows mirroring the world back on the rest of the neighborhood.

Inside, there is a room for every need: a foyer, a living room, a dining room, a family room, a laundry room, a play room. There are two bathrooms upstairs and another two downstairs. There is a deck that overlooks the woods, a whirlpool tub, and four bedrooms with roomy closets. Only the basement remains unfinished, concrete and cold.

Your bedroom is in the back of the house with huge windows that look out into the woods. The view is quiet and private, with sun streaming between the trees.

Your father's money keeps coming in. He buys a silver Porsche and drives it up and down the steep driveway. On the school bus, kids stare when they find out the "mansion on the hill" is yours. You learn not to brag about where you live.

The house is never more itself than on Halloween. It stands dark and threatening in the air that is thick with sugar and screams. A single flickering pumpkin stands at the ready on the porch. It is a long and cold trek all the way up to the house, but trick-or-treaters still come. No one throws eggs or toilet paper. They are afraid of the house, afraid of what it might do when their backs are turned.

You are afraid too, though you'd never admit it. You heard somewhere that more murders are committed in cul-de-sacs than on regular streets. The big house makes noises at night, noises that keep you up and make you cry, but you wake in the morning with sunlight easing through your pull-down shades. It is on one morning like this that you discover you can open the side window in your room and step outside to sit on the roof. You have to be careful, or your mother will yell. You sit in the sun on the roof and look at the trees and the backyard. There is no one else in sight.

For twelve years you live in this house. It is where you get your first period and your first kiss. In high school, when you start driving, you too go up and down that long driveway. Your father, though, is no longer there. He lives on the coast now, with another woman and even another dog. But you've got school and your friends and the new dog Brady, a great big Australian shepherd. You have your mother, who stays alone in the empty house when you are out with friends. When you come home late at night she is standing in the dimly lit foyer, waiting for you.

Dorm Room

It is bigger than you expected, or at least that's what you tell your-self. In reality, it's large enough only to hold two single beds and two small desks built into the wall, each flanked by a wardrobe that maintains the scent of its previous residents. You choose the bed by the window and dress it up with the new purple bedspread, a cheap one from a discount store, bought on impulse because you went shopping by yourself and didn't know there were warmer options. You tape to the walls pictures torn from magazines, snapshots of your high school friends. You are alone; your mother was sick and could not help you move in.

Your roommate has curly hair and a big personality. At first she seems worldly and confident, but before long she reveals herself to be scared and insecure. Just like you. Sometimes the two of you fight, and at other times you stay awake to talk and laugh in the dark. At these times, you could be in any house or bedroom in your history. They're all the same.

At the end of the spring semester, you move out of the dorm room to go home for the summer. The money has dried up, but the house is still there. So is your mother, but she has lost weight and complains of pains in her abdomen. Some nights, you both sleep downstairs in the living room. Neither of you say it, but it's because you're both afraid. In the middle of the night you wake and search for your mother. There she is, breathing softly. You lie on your back and stare at the vaulted ceiling of the living room, the peak that in seasons past was brushed by the tips of Christmas trees. On impulse, you sit up to make sure she is still breathing, still dreaming. An hour later you check again, watching her chest rise and fall. You expect you'll be checking all night long for the rest of your life.

First Apartment

Your first apartment after college is a one-bedroom with parquet floors and a balcony overlooking a parking lot. You set it on fire your first night there, while trying to operate the gas stove. The fire department comes and sets up big fans inside to blow out the horrible smoke smell. You end up sitting on the steps outside the garden-style units, clutching a cat carrier and crying. This is how you meet your neighbors, but after that night you never speak to them again, and in fact they seem to disappear. You know no one in this city. The apartment management has to put you in the display unit until your apartment can be repaired.

You move back in before long. There are three locks on the door and a gate for the sliding glass balcony door. Just in case. At night you make dinner alone and sprinkle catnip on the floors. You miss the Australian shepherd. You miss feeling safe in suburbia, you miss getting in your car and knowing where all the roads will take you.

Mostly, you miss your mother. At night, before you doze off under the pale glow from the streetlights outside, you pretend she is still back in the mansion on the hill, working in the garden, walking the dog. You pretend she is happy, healthy. You pretend she is still alive.

Cobblestone Street

Your career advances along like a dutiful ant overtaking the leaf. You move to a bigger, fancier city, in a waterfront condo that features exposed brick walls and all new appliances. You order gourmet coffee from the shop downstairs and browse the corner bookstore on the weekends. Money comes and goes easily, painlessly. You work long hours and sometimes walk the streets alone at night, the ground turning to cobblestones just before you reach your neighborhood.

This goes on for a few years. New wrinkles, as dainty and unsure as pre-teens, appear around your eyes. You do the math and realize your mother already had a young teenager by this age. But you have a cosmopolitan lifestyle, a flush bank account, and a condo that is cleaned twice weekly by a service that leaves little mints on your kitchen counter. You eat them in the morning on the way to work, savoring the sharp, cold taste.

Marriage Bed

It starts by him moving into your waterfront condo, but as the years pass the space feels too tight and you start considering getting a dog together. Or maybe two dogs. And then the wedding, a modest courthouse affair for which you wear an old blue dress that belonged to your mother. Its skirts fall like sheer memories, the silvery band stretched across your waist. Your new husband wears his nicest suit, and afterward, you go out for coffee and pastries and discuss moving plans. Your possessions fit inside one large truck. The new house is on the outskirts of the city, still accessible via the light-rail line. You want an Australian shepherd and your husband wants a beagle, but you compromise by going to the shelter and getting a medium-sized mutt with hair that tangles above his eyes.

The house is a three bedroom, much smaller than the mansion on the hill, but it is warm and compact and well designed. You prepare food on the island in the kitchen and work your way into the cramped basement to do laundry. The master bedroom is your favorite part of the whole house. Your husband surprised you with an antique bed frame, and from the posts you hang strands of fake flowered vines that emit a kind of dusty message. You throw an old comforter of your mother's across the bottom of the bed and admire the red and brown stitching as if she had sewn it herself.

This becomes home, the bed your link to family and eventually, the lone happy symbol of your marriage. After several years, you are grateful you kept your job in the city. The divorce is messy, mostly because you fight over the dog. He ends up winning that battle but you get the bed, that heavy flowered frame you eventually leave behind when you move into a smaller place.

The Watch Factory

You never could have predicted this, to end up back in your hometown. You grew up in the suburbs but now live downtown in an historic apartment building. Sometimes you drive through the countryside, the suburbs, and inevitably end up driving past both of your old houses. First the modest one, with the picture window and the porch where you pretended to be a lion. The neighborhood has descended into disrepair. Piles of junk teeter on the porch, and a rough chain-link fence stakes its claim on the property line. You slow your car but do not stop or get out for fear of the barking dogs nearby, the ones who appear to have been trained through mistreatment.

The other house, the mansion on the hill, is more or less as you remembered it, except now its flat, glassy profile appears somber instead of threatening and superior. The landscaping is well kept, better than when it was your family's responsibility. The only other evidence you can detect of the new owners is the mailbox, a cartoonish-green plastic thing, and a little flowering tree in the front yard. You wonder why that tree lived and the dogwoods your parents planted all those years ago did not. Maybe the soil has something more to it now. Maybe it gained nourishment with age.

You slow your car in the cul-de-sac and drive around once, twice, three times. You are reluctant to stop, and on your fifth time around you force yourself to turn the wheel and keep driving.

Back in your apartment, at night, you listen to the noises in the walls. Decades ago, this was a watchmaking factory. The lower level is made out like a maze. Pipes run along the ceiling, and it is so cold. You always shiver on the way through the halls, and not just from the temperature. The building is old, the factory was dangerous. People died here, in these walls. At night you lie awake and think: Someday I will, too.

The Sixth Floor

You are not old enough for this disease. Everyone says this, from the doctors to the nurses to the few friends you have in town. They say it might not be terminal but you know your fate. This is the same hospital your mother died in, just two floors down. You remember the place at the end of her hallway where you found a phone and called your best friend to give her the news. You stayed on that phone for almost an hour. It had a little sign that said *For nurses only*, but no one stopped you.

Now you are in a room on the sixth floor, with a roommate named Monica and a window overlooking the parking lot. You had an apartment, once, overlooking a parking lot. And then there were cobblestones, and a bed frame, and a factory that produced time. So much time, rolling down the conveyer, the workers standing back to watch its measured march.

You drift, you doze. Monica never answers when you call her. The curtains move in the breeze but then you remember that the window does not open, that the drapes are heavy and thick and not pale wispy veils that twist in the sunlight.

All of Thereafter

In the end, it's nothing to fear. Some darkness, a stretch of quiet, and then light. Your biggest disappointment is the loneliness. It's just like living. Worse, your mother is nowhere to be found. You thought you'd at least have that.

Before long, you discover that you are able to go anywhere, to revisit anything in your life. You walk into the house in New York, the caterpillar house with the interior you were too young to remember. But you know it now, as if the nine-month-old you stored memories like carefully packed boxes. There is the kitchen, the family room, the corner where your mother nursed you. And the outside, of course: the dog run, the brick walls that had been covered with caterpillars, the grass your mother set you down on during nice days.

Next is the white house, the porch of the lions. It is such a different experience from those times you drove by when you were still alive. Now you can go inside and crawl into that little room under the stairs, or sit in the picture window, or lie down on the multicolored shag carpeting. It is all the same now as it was then, right down to the macramé owl hanging. The kitchen table, a cheap false wood one with leaves, is still there, with an ashtray full of your father's cigarette butts.

You move on to the mansion on the hill, where you walk through the empty rooms. Your bedroom is still pale purple, your mother's chest of drawers still contains that secret compartment where she kept her best jewelry. You walk back downstairs again and find that you are crying. You are crying because what you see isn't the house at all but you: young and growing, alive.

You could go on to the dorm rooms, the apartments, the house you shared with your husband. You could go to all these places in the span of a breath, but you feel rooted here, as rooted as a spirit can be. As you pace the dining room, remembering long-ago Thanksgivings and the way your mother carried the turkey platter to the table, you realize that if every person has one true home, this must be yours.

You leave through the back door and wander outside in the yard, near the edge of the woods. It smells the same, that crisp scent of leaves and grass and soil. There, by the woodpile, you once saw a black snake winding its way through the grass, and there is the path in the woods where you played as a child.

Then you notice movement among the trees, and the branches part to reveal Brady, the Australian shepherd. He runs to you, alive and warm and thrilled. He jumps up, his paws against your chest. You pet him all over, scratch his head, and cry again.

When the two of you finally calm down, you turn in a slow circle, Brady at your side. The woods are quiet. No one else appears. You close your eyes against the wind and tell yourself that when you reopen them, she will be standing in front of you.

Brady lets out a little whine. You open your eyes. The world stretches out before you, on and on and on. Brady moves at your side; he is restless, too. You rest a hand on his head and tell him that sometimes, there is nothing to do but wait. If you spend a lifetime and all of thereafter waiting, you might get to see her emerge alive and shimmering through the trees.

Live Model

People say I look just like Melanie St. Clair, the famous television actress. If you're thinking, "How nice, she looks like a TV star," then you must be in the one percent of the population that doesn't know who Melanie St. Clair is. So let me fill you in: In addition to being the star of the hit hospital drama *Intensive Care*, Melanie St. Clair is ugly. Her face brings to mind the unlikely love match of an anteater and a baby hippopotamus. Pointing out that someone looks like Melanie St. Clair is not a compliment. It's an attack.

On the other hand, Melanie St. Clair's career is proof that you don't have to be pretty, or even passably plain, to become a success. Not that I do anything even remotely as exciting as acting. I work at Clandestine Claudia's, the lingerie store on

Fourth and Sunnydale. Picture a Victoria's Secret, only a little less expensive and not quite so nice. Our store colors are lavender and silver instead of that predictable pink at Vicky's, and we fill each pale-purple shopping bag with loads of silvery confetti that will plague your home for days when all you wanted was a few pairs of sale-priced underwear.

I've worked at Claudia's for nearly two years now. God knows why they hired me in the first place, seeing as how you'd expect only beautiful women to work in a lingerie store. My theory is that I prevent the men from getting worked up around all the underwear and sexy mannequins. They start to sweat and then look over and see me and immediately come back to earth.

Plus, the store owner, Lucille Pennysworth, is fat. I mean really fat, like the kind of body you see in photographs accompanying obesity articles. Since all the other employees are relatively attractive, maybe she wanted me as her partner in ugly. Either way, I'm here to stay. My job primarily consists of running the cash register, untangling skinny plastic bra hangers, and measuring customers to determine their optimal bra size.

But my comfortable routine is about to change. It all started last week, when Lucille was struck with her "fabulous" and "revolutionary" idea of live window modeling. She approached me while I was wrestling the new line of polka-dotted separates back into place on the rack.

"I was thinking," Lucille said as she wandered over, tapping her fat fingers against her fat chin, "that maybe you could do a little modeling for us."

"Me? A model?" I imagined my face in a newspaper ad, or maybe even in the local Clandestine Claudia's mailer. They'd have to use a hell of a lot of Vaseline on the camera lens to make that work.

"It's this idea I had," Lucille went on. She was starting to get excited. I could tell by the way the fat jiggled on her neck. "If we could get a live model to stand in our store window wearing our product, then think of all the attention we'd get!" Lucille always insisted on referring to the underwear we sold as "product."

"And you want me to be the one to do this?"

Lucille nodded. She looked satisfied with herself. So satisfied, in fact, that I felt guilty saying anything but yes. Lucille is not such a bad person, as far as people go, and at times I even have the urge to make her happy. It did seem a bit strange she would ask me, of all people, to model, but I should point out that despite my face, I have a pretty fantastic body. Size four with just enough hips-butt-boobs to avoid looking like a stick.

I should also mention that Lucille didn't ask anyone else to model. She excluded all the pretty girls, the prettiest of whom is Penelope Gardner, a tall woman with deep-black skin, high cheek-bones, and tiny feet that she likes to wear in ballet flats with the ribbon wrapped up around her calves. Crazy attire is encouraged at Clandestine Claudia's. Lucille thought that our wacky outfits might entice customers to come in if only to see what the heck we were wearing that day. Unfortunately, Lucille isn't always a fan of my concoctions—I favor floppy overalls covering t-shirts air-brushed with photos of golden retrievers, or loosely woven palm leaf hats that flake off all over the lavender carpeting. Who knows, maybe this is why she wanted me to strip most of the way down and stand in front of our store window for hours at a time.

So I agreed to do it, and now today is my first day in my new role as live model. I close myself into the dressing room and put on the matching set Lucille picked out for me: a deep purple push-up bra with boy-cut panties trimmed in silver lace. It's straight off the display rack, and I get to keep it at the end of the day. That's a bonus to modeling underwear: you can't exactly put it back on the rack when you're done.

I adjust the bra and make three turns in front of the mirror in the tiny lavender-painted dressing room. Then I go and stand in the window.

What is being a live lingerie model like? I will tell you. It is painful and boring and kind of thrilling. For the first half hour I stand more or less in the same position, mimicking our real mannequins: one leg slightly in front of the other with my hands splayed palm-up in front of me, like I'm posing in front of a car at an auto show. I arch my feet as much as I can and smile at the people walking outside on the street.

At first, no one takes much notice. I must look like a real mannequin, and this somehow makes me proud. I stretch and move around a bit. After a few more minutes, Lucille comes striding around the corner, almost knocking over a rack of paisley-printed bras. They are the kind of bras I prefer because they have no padding, the straps don't cut into your skin, and the clasp is in the front.

"How's it going?" Lucille smiles through her makeup, which I notice is starting to get greasy on her face. "Getting tired? Have you been standing this whole time?"

"Going good, Lucille," I say. "I really think this is going to work out."

Lucille beams but what I actually meant was that I was happy about the free underwear. Then I remember that I should have asked for a raise; being a model is surely more specialized work than running the cash register. It feels too late to ask now. I imagine Melanie St. Clair is the same way, letting bigger offers slip by. Probably even her agent knows not to ask too much for her face.

"Here. I brought you this." Lucille holds up a folding chair. "It'll kill your feet to stand in one place all day. So every now and then you can have a seat."

Lucille helps me unfold the chair and stick it in the corner. She looks at me and sighs. "To be young again," she says wistfully, and then shuffles off. What could she mean by that? Surely Lucille was never a size four. If she was, then she needs to write a gossipy book about how all those pounds came on. Seriously. People love reading that stuff.

I shift around a bit. There's an air conditioning vent over the window and chilly air blasts down onto me. I'll probably get a stiff neck. I reach up and pull my hair down around my shoulders—I have this absolutely amazing, super long brown hair—and wonder whether I can file a workers' comp claim if the exposure to cold air makes me sick.

No. I could never do that to Lucille.

The day wears on. Slowly, people start to notice that the girl in the window is not, in fact, your typical mannequin. I guess it's my face that tips them off. I watch as people nudge each other and point in my direction. Some come right up to the window to peer at me. It's like being a gerbil at the pet store—a half-naked gerbil wearing nice underthings, but a gerbil nonetheless.

Around 11 A.M., I get my first through-the-window comparison: A passerby mouths what looks exactly like "Mel-an-nie St.

Clair" to his friend. They both look amazed, like they have seen something special.

ꚘꚘꚘꚘꚘ

On the second day I wear a pink and black bra with black silk panties. Then it's a matching orange set, and the day after that Lucille gets daring and puts me in a tan ensemble that matches my skin tone so closely that from a distance, I look like I'm naked.

A funny thing starts to happen. People see me in the window and gravitate toward the store. They come in. They start buying bras and underwear at such a rate that it's like half the city has a hot date this very night.

At first, Lucille let me put on clothes now and then and go back to measuring customers or straightening the display racks, but as more people come into the store based on my modeling, she asks me to stay there as long as I can stand it. She even buys one of those vibrating floor pads to help the circulation in my feet.

Today I'm wearing a stretchy, dark-blue cotton set. It's one of my favorites because it's simple and soft and brings out my eyes. One thing most people don't notice, by the way, is that Melanie St. Clair has brown eyes and mine are blue. It always surprises me that no one picks up on this. I guess the rest of the face is too important.

I'm busy deciding on my next pose when I notice a commotion outside. A Channel 4 News van pulls up in the no-parking zone in front of the store, and all the people who had been milling around turn to stare at the van. I wonder if someone robbed the bank down the street, or if there's a fire or a car accident. But no. They are training the camera on me.

The cameraman positions himself only a few feet away from the window. No one gives me any direction, and I'm not sure what to do. So I pose. I turn to the side, bend my knees, stick my butt out a little, and put my hands on my thighs. Then I turn my face to the window and smile a huge smile.

"Lucille," I call out through my teeth. "Channel 4 is here."

"What?" I hear her thundering toward the window, but I refuse to break my pose to turn to look at her. "What in the world?" Lucille says behind me, and then she hurries out the door.

I can see her now, standing on the sidewalk, talking to the Channel 4 crew. She gestures in my direction a few times, then wrings her hands. Finally, she starts nodding her head, up down up down. When she comes back inside, a blond woman in a gray skirt suit and a flashy red blouse follows her.

Now there's a sizeable crowd outside the windows, the biggest we've seen since I started live modeling. The camera is still rolling. I consider sticking out my tongue but decide that is probably not the image Clandestine Claudia's wants to portray.

"Here she is," I hear Lucille say behind me. I can smell strong vanilla perfume, which is not Lucille's scent. Must be the suited lady.

"Excuse me," a voice says. I think I recognize it from the 5 o'clock news. "Margaret?"

Yes, fine. My name is Margaret. An ugly name to match my ugly face.

"It's okay," Lucille says, "you can turn around." To the news lady she whispers, "Isn't she professional?"

I stand up straight, which is a relief because frankly that pose was killing my back, and turn to look at the anchor lady. Sherry

O'Connor, that's her name. I remember now. She reaches to shake my hand. She must be wearing about ten rings. On each hand.

"We want to do a story on this," Sherry says, waving to the store in general. "On your window modeling."

"Okay."

"Great!" She waves the cameraman inside. "We already got some exterior shots. Now Gene will film you inside while I ask you some questions. All right?"

"Okay."

While Gene and Sherry determine the best angle, Penelope Gardner passes by. She looks pissed. But she can't glower for long because a customer is asking her questions about the heart-print negligees in the corner. I look after them almost wistfully, thinking of simpler days.

"Ready," Sherry says. She musters up a big fake smile and starts a rapid monologue about innovative marketing concepts, shock factor, sex appeal. Then she turns to me. "Margaret, what's it like to model underwear all day long in front of strangers?"

They already told me not to look directly into the camera, but I can't help it. I'm drawn to it. I wonder if this is how Melanie St. Clair felt the first time she was filmed.

"Oh, I love it," I tell the camera, and I smile. But my answer feels insufficient, so I try to think of something else, fast. "It encourages people to go window shopping," I add. "And that, um, can be good for the economy."

"Do you ever get self-conscious?"

I shrug. "Not really. People spend all day judging each other, anyway. I'm just making it a little easier for them."

Sherry tilts her head back and laughs like a dragon. Then she leans in closer, like we're finally about to get personal.

"Has anyone ever told you," she breathes, "that you look exactly like Melanie St. Clair?"

Oh good God. She asked that question on camera. It would be on the news!

I shake my head as if to clear it. Out of the corner of my eye, I can see even more people gathering outside, pointing.

"Why, no," I tell Sherry O'Connor. "No, I have never heard that before. But thank you. I'm so flattered you think so."

Sherry grins. When she's done with her questions and Gene has stopped filming, she shakes my hand again. "A pleasure," she says, pumping my arm up and down. "A real pleasure."

They leave and Lucille lets me take a break to revel in the excitement of my first television interview. When I come back from the break room, the store is more crowded than I have ever seen it. It's going to be a nightmare untangling all the bra hangers tonight.

As I walk toward the window, people poke each other and say, "There she is!" A few wave, and I wave back. The story hasn't even hit Channel 4 yet.

In the window, I strike a new pose: one hand up on the wall, my face tilted to the left, the curve of my body sliding to the right. I maintain my expression—slightly playful, like I'm on the verge of a wink—as more people gather on the sidewalk to stare at me.

Who knew I'd be such a good actress?

I'm in the newspaper, too. And on Channel 7, and even Channel 10, which I have always considered the classiest of the three local news stations. Earlier today, a handful of men in suits came in, and Lucille swept them into her office in the back. There is talk of opening additional stores, franchises, investors flush with start-up funds. All of a sudden, everyone believes in Claudia's.

Lucille walks around on the lavender-colored carpet with stars in her eyes all day long. She cancels the anything-goes dress code and buys uniforms: sleeved lavender mini-dresses with wide lapels and shiny silver buttons. Everyone wears the new dresses except me, because I model underwear, and Lucille, who is too fat for a mini-dress. She starts showing up in expensive-looking pantsuits with colorful silk scarves at her neck. I've never seen her look so pretty.

On top of all that, I finally got my raise. Lucille upped my salary from $9 an hour to $12.25 without my even asking. I happen to know that as head cashier, Penelope makes $11.40.

I'm painting a pretty picture, but it's not all so great. Some customers get the idea it would be fun to stand behind me and whisper nasty comments, or to throw lint or straw wrappers at my barely clad behind. All this makes Lucille hire a store security guard. "I have to protect my girls," she says firmly. Sheesh. A few weeks of tripled sales, and she's talking like the housemother for a bordello.

The security guard's name is Al. He stands behind me with his arms crossed and a mean look on his face, but it's all for show. When no one else is around, he whispers knock-knock jokes under his breath to keep me entertained. Al has a wife and a five-year-old daughter and is thankful to have the Claudia's job because times have been hard in our little city for quite a while now.

At noon, when Al and I head back to the break room for

lunch, Penelope steps in front of us. She's carrying an armload of mail.

"Look what I have," she says. For a woman with cheekbones that go from here to Alabama, you'd think she would be above smirking. "Three to one," Penelope says. "That's the ratio of hate mail to fan mail today."

She thrusts a pile into my hands. The letters are already open, of course. I know without looking what kinds of things they will say. They will mention my face, how extraordinarily ugly I am, how I'm a disgrace to the town and shouldn't be allowed outside, much less modeling in a public place. People actually wake up in the morning, have some corn flakes, then sit down at their breakfast nooks and write letters like this to strangers. To me.

I pass the letters over to Al, who takes them without a word and dumps them in the trash. God love him. "You know, Penelope, Lucille might let you model, too," I say. "Maybe if you beg."

She smiles, showing big straight white teeth a girl like me could only dream of. "No chance," she says. "People only come here because they can't believe someone like you is on display." She glances around at all the customers, some of whom are indeed peering from behind bra racks to stare at me. "You're a freak show."

Al steps between us, just like in the movies. "I think that's enough, Penelope," he says in his low voice. Al must be a great dad. When his daughter is a teenager he'll have no problem handling her boyfriends.

Penelope shrugs and starts toward the cash register. Halfway there, she turns back. "Enjoy this while you can," she advises. "You'll never get this much attention again in your entire life."

Al takes my arm and moves me toward the break room. I trail him silently, and even though I packed my favorite sandwich—peanut butter and lettuce, with a few potato chips smashed on top—I'm no longer hungry. Because Penelope, despite her ridiculous beauty and her inability to multiply in her head, is right. And I know it.

჻ ჻ ჻

Our little city has gone into an absolute spasm of excitement. Melanie St. Clair herself has learned about Clandestine Claudia's and my modeling. Someone showed her pictures of my face, proof that she is not alone in this world, and now she wants to come here and see for herself. She's going to fly from L.A. to come meet me, to see if I really am every inch as ugly as she is.

There's some business to conduct, as well. Lucille says Melanie St. Clair might be interested in being the spokesperson for a regional media campaign for the store, which could lay the groundwork for national commercials once Claudia's is franchised and operating all over the southeast and eventually, the entire nation.

You'd think with all this success that a few new opportunities would come my way, like a commercial offer or even a lousy print ad, but they haven't. Not even one.

Melanie St. Clair is due to make a public appearance late tomorrow morning at Claudia's. She'll come stand in the window with me—she'll be fully clothed, of course—and we'll both wave to the window shoppers. Then she'll sit at a table in the back of the store and sign autographs for her many fans.

When I first heard Melanie St. Clair was coming to our city,

I imagined her entrance would be dramatic: Like she arrives in a helicopter and everyone has to hold on to their hats and hairdos while straining into the wind to catch a glance of the famous television actress, an ugly woman who manages to become beautiful in the glowing adoration of a crowd.

In reality, she's flying in from L.A. late at night, going straight to a hotel, and then having an early meeting with Lucille and some investors at the store before it opens. Lucille invited me, too, and of course I accepted. This is Melanie St. Clair we're talking about.

I get up early in the morning, way earlier than necessary, and stand in front of my closet for a long while. I've hung all my new bra-and-panty sets on their little plastic hangers, so my closet is starting to look like a lingerie store. I run my hand over them, listening to the tinkling of the plastic. The padded bras move stiffly; the thin ones flutter and fall back into place. Choosing among them feels almost painful, so I compromise by choosing an emerald-green bra from one set and a pair of black sequined undies from another. I lay them both out on the bed, leaving their hangers drifting empty on the clothing bar.

Then I pull out my best dress, which unfortunately is an orange-and-white-striped cotton shift that is essentially a long rectangle. Also, it has a slight mustard stain just to the left of my heart. But it will have to do. I shower and comb my hair until my scalp hurts, and then I get dressed and play around with my makeup bag for a while before giving up and leaving my face bare. It doesn't matter what I do; I will always look like her.

I usually take the bus to work, but since Claudia's is only two miles away and it's still early, I decide to walk. I put on a big pair of black sunglasses in hopes that no one will recognize me on the way. Since my newfound fame, I've had to endure some nasty comments on the street. And while a few people have asked for my autograph, I could never tell whether they were being sarcastic. I went ahead and signed anyway, figuring it was their problem if they didn't really want my signature.

It's nice to be up so early in the morning. The air feels clean, and shadows bob across the sidewalks. The streets are deserted, and I take my time ambling along. When I'm almost to the store, several people turn a corner in front of me, heading in my direction. I stop, squinting.

It's her. It's Melanie St. Clair, walking toward the store entrance with a modest entourage of people who will follow her to the ends of the earth no matter what her face looks like, so long as she stays famous. She, too, is wearing sunglasses. But she's also wearing a crisp beige dress belted at the waist, an armful of skinny gold bracelets, and shoes that are probably real crocodile or snake or whatever type of lizard they make shoes from. She must have seen me at the same time, because she has also stopped in her tracks.

"You're Melanie St. Clair," I say, as if I'm on some sort of game show and I was asked to identify a celebrity.

Melanie St. Clair smiles, but it looks forced. "Well. You must be Margaret." She has a slight British accent, though I know she's American through and through.

Before I can ask about the accent, she takes off her sunglasses. I figure it would be rude not to do the same, so I take mine off as well. And there we are. I would say it's like looking into a mirror, but that would not be entirely true. Melanie St. Clair is better dressed than I am. She's wearing artfully applied makeup, her skin glows a Californian bronze, and even her expression is the stiff superior one of a winner. She is very unattractive, but she is something else: entirely, wholly herself. I am nothing but ugly.

We have a little standoff there on the sidewalk, baring our nearly identical faces. I'm wondering what we could possibly have to say to each other when Lucille comes running up to us. Or at least she's moving as fast as she can, which might be more of a lumber than anything else, but still. She's out of breath.

"The store," she gasps, heaving herself along. I turn and take a few steps closer to the store entrance, and for the first time I notice a scattering of glass shards on the sidewalk. It's quite pretty, actually. The pieces glow pink and blue in the light, like confetti still falling in a parade.

"Wait a second." I step back. "That's my window." The window Melanie St. Clair and I are supposed to stand behind in a few short hours. The window that made me famous, protecting me from the street crowds while my neck grew stiff from the air conditioning.

Melanie St. Clair walks up to the broken window on her high heels. She bends down and peers in, wrinkling her long skinny nose. "What bad luck," she says.

Lucille laughs, the high, uncontained laugh of someone about to go over the edge. "Oh, they didn't choose our store by chance. It was quite intentional." She wrenches a ring of keys out of her purse and goes to open the front door, though frankly the hole in the window is nearly big enough for even her to get through. Melanie St. Clair and I follow her through the door.

If I had stopped long enough to consider what might have happened inside this store, it would still be worse than I imagined. All the racks are knocked to the floor, with bras scattered like casualties. Entire panty displays were wiped clean, the underwear hanging off mannequins' heads or tied tight to the light fixtures. But those are the petty crimes. The vandals had obtained dark purple and red spray paint, probably from the hardware store down the street, and they also may have used the services of the copy center two blocks away to blow up photographs from the paper. Lucille and I are plastered there on the wall, our features huge and hideous.

Do I really need to go into detail describing what those spray-painted words say? It's exactly as unoriginal as you'd imagine. "Whale" is scripted next to Lucille's face, "Dog" next to mine. The wall behind the cash registers boldly declares, "Ugly bitches work here," which isn't fair to the other Clandestine Claudia's girls, most of whom are downright attractive.

"Oh," Lucille says, looking around at her defiled lavender store. She starts that game of blinking as fast as she can to stop the tears. This goes to show that even sudden and thrilling business success can't make a person immune to hurt feelings.

Melanie St. Clair puts her arm on Lucille's shoulder. This surprises me; in the few short moments I've been with Melanie St. Clair, I've already slated her as the coldest woman in the world.

"Now, Lucille," she says, as if she and my boss have been best friends since grade school, "it will be all right."

"It won't," Lucille insists. The tears are starting to come now, cutting muddy lines through all that foundation she wears. "The investors are meeting here," she sputters. "And the camera crews and the reporters. We have news crews coming from three cities away."

Melanie St. Clair rubs her hand up and down Lucille's arm. "This happens," she says with a shrug. "People like us have to put up with this kind of garbage every day for our whole lives." She looks over at me. "You know what I mean?"

I feel like my insides are shrinking. I look at the word *dog* next to my face, complete with a big arrow clarifying the target. I've been called worse things, in public, and in front of people I care about. One time someone threw a milkshake at me in the park. It mostly missed but I still had to go home and change my shirt. My friend Janine was with me that day, and I made a big joke about it, explaining that my shirt was so far out of style it was trying to commit fashion suicide, and I better go change. Another time, when my mother was in town, we were having lunch at an outdoor café when two college guys started making fun of me as they walked past. I had to sit there pretending I didn't hear them while my mother signaled for the check. And I won't even get into what my school years were like.

Standing there on the lavender carpet, with glass scattered near my window, I can see this abuse will never stop, not even if I one day become as famous as Melanie St. Clair. Not even if I become her.

There's a crunch of glass outside, and then the door swings open and Al comes storming in. Penelope slinks in behind him.

"What the hell?" Al bellows. He rushes over to my side. "You okay?"

"I'm fine." I can't take my eyes off Penelope, who is staring wordlessly at the destruction. "What are *you* doing here?"

She looks at me, surprised. "I came to watch the interviews," she says. "God, this is awful."

"Damn right it is." Al stomps around, inspecting the damage. "Lucille, you should have let me work out 24/7 security."

"What's the difference," I mutter. "When they probably had keys anyway."

Penelope pulls back. "What?"

Al is leaning over a pile of bras that have been freed from their plastic hangers and are lying crumpled on the floor. He picks one up gingerly; the underwire has broken through and pierced the padding. He gently pushes at the wire, trying to urge it back in.

I turn to Lucille, who is drying her eyes with a lavender tissue. "This was a mistake," I tell her. "You never should have had me model in the first place."

Lucille sniffles. "I wanted to give you a chance."

A chance. So even Lucille pitied me. And here's Penelope, actually looking sorry for me, and Al already tearing the photos from the wall. There will always be people who think these horrible things about me, whether they show it through insults or keep quiet and kind.

I slide away and make my way back to the break room, which has been spared what the rest of the store suffered. I barely glance at the dull green and yellow linoleum, the mismatched line of coat hooks, and the vending machines that sport Twizzlers and terrible coffee. I go right to my own locker and pull out whatever I have in there: a set of clothes, a CD I once lent to another employee, and finally my silver nametag with the tiny heart on the right side.

I take the silver weight in my hand and walk right out of the break room. If I hurry, I can catch the next bus. If I walk fast enough through the store, maybe I won't even look back.

ﾞﾞﾞﾞﾞ

I make the bus just in time and find a seat in the back. I wish I had some music so I could listen to something sad. Instead, I glance around and see a young man sitting across the aisle from me. He has a drawing pad on his lap and is busy sketching a girl sitting sideways a few seats ahead of him. If you saw this girl on a bus or on the street, you wouldn't think twice about her. She's neither ugly nor beautiful. Just a regular, normal girl. How often I've wanted to be someone exactly like her.

But a funny thing happens. In the man's drawing, this girl becomes something special. He sketches her hair, somehow making the long pencil strokes look soft and bright on the page. He makes the side of her face smooth, blissful. He spends a lot of time on the details of her ear. And I realize that she looks so beautiful not because he's altering her image, but because he's paying attention to her without her knowledge. She's sitting on the bus, traveling somewhere, thinking her own thoughts, while he is devoting every bit of his concentration to her. She will live forever in the sketchbook of a stranger, and she doesn't even know it.

At first I find it unbearable that she isn't aware of what is happening. The bus passes my stop but I stay on, watching this girl who has no idea she is being watched, being recorded. I could get up and tell her. I could point to the picture and she would realize that sometimes we live in places we never knew existed, like in the tip of a charcoal pencil or in the admiration in a young artist's mind.

Then I decide it is better to let the world make such small

kindnesses, like the love created by one stranger sketching another on a bus. This way, the girl in the drawing could be everything the viewer expects and more. She could be smart, she could be playful, she could be kind. She could be me.

The Clarinet

When I asked my mother if she would still teach me the clarinet had I been born a boy, she told me of course not, these lessons are for girls. She said one day I would have a daughter and teach her, too. That was when I learned how to put an instrument together, how to connect it piece by piece, and also how to resist: I decided on the spot that I would grow up and have only boys, who could play trumpet or snare drum or maybe even nothing at all.

She handed me the clarinet then. It was black with sparks of silver and it felt solid, alive. I tapped my fingers down the front, covering each hole and touching keys that curved from the sides like stiff wings. I thought of all the air running from the mouthpiece to the bottom of the bell, and how the force of my breath could somehow make song. Then I brought it to my lips and started to play.

That was three years ago, when I was in the third grade. No one else in my class played an instrument yet, but my mother said if I practiced every day I could become the best, like she had been. Of course, she once said the same thing to my sister Shelly, who turned out to be a sloppy player. Shelly never practiced, faked it during concerts, and used a lighter to singe the ends of her reeds.

But as my mother says, I was a different story. I breezed through the beginner books so fast I thought she would cry. I got into the intermediate band when I was still in fifth grade, which hasn't happened for a clarinetist in this school district in nearly three decades. On Thursday afternoons I walked from the elementary school to the middle school for band practice, carrying the clarinet case like a ticket.

She called me a prodigy. When the band director held auditions and I won first chair, I started to believe her.

⬥⬥⬥⬥⬥⬥

My mother has had this clarinet since she was eight years old. It is a Buffet Crampon, a professional model manufactured in France. It is made out of genuine wood and still has its original hard case lined in deep blue velvet. I take pleasure in opening this case and running my hands over the velvet, picking up the clarinet pieces and placing them back again. I am lucky for the chance to play an instrument of quality, durability, and pureness of sound.

My classmates play cheap plastic clarinets bought from the mega music store in town, or worse, they rent instruments from school that come in banged-up cases lined in thinning, off-red velvet. My mother's clarinet sounds richer and fuller than theirs. When I play I consider the instrument's craftsmanship, its history, and the love my mother put into it all those years ago. I also play with the understanding that no matter how good I become, this clarinet will still belong to her.

Everyone else in band takes lessons from either the band director or a private instructor in town, but my mother teaches me. We sit on my bed and pull a music stand toward our knees. My mother opens the lesson book and sounds out funny words, like *straw-berr-y,* to demonstrate rhythm. Today I get distracted because I'm picturing myself in high school, wearing a uniform and marching on a soggy football field while the glittering baton girls wait on the sidelines. My mother taps at the music stand and tells me to focus. I take a breath and start at the top of the sheet music. I wouldn't look good in sequins, anyway. Once a girl at school called me a giraffe, and that's not the kind of thing you grow out of.

After the lesson, my mother leaves so I can practice alone. I practice for an hour every day, more on weekends. Today I lose track of time, playing for an extra twenty minutes without even realizing it. My mother notices when she passes my room and says that's good, keep going, because seating auditions are in a week and I need to hold on to first chair.

Shelly has been away at college for three months now, and we haven't heard from her in almost two weeks. My mother has taken to calling her dorm room in the middle of the night, but either no one answers or the roommate picks up and says that Shelly is out for the evening, please stop calling.

I would drive out there and check up on her, my mother says, if it wouldn't affect your practice time.

My practice time is apparently delicate. It relies on three nice meals with vegetables every day, plenty of sleep, and a strict schedule. Traveling two states away with my mother to check on Shelly would only disturb my rhythm and possibly make me lose first chair to Tameka, who is a year older but has so far been incapable of dethroning me.

Tameka and I got into a reed war earlier this year. Clarinet reeds come in different sizes, going from soft to hard as their numbers increase. Tameka got the idea that only the best players could use the higher numbers, so she and I each showed up with harder and harder reeds until we were both on fives and sounded terrible. The director encouraged us to call a truce, so I went back to a three-and-a-half reed while Tameka went back to a number three.

The reed is attached to the mouthpiece by a piece of metal called the ligature. The ligature is easily bent if stepped on, whether by accident or on purpose, as Mark Cooley did last year after I rejected his offer to hold hands on the bus. Even now he sometimes comes up behind me in the band room and hits the small of my back with his trombone slide. I ignore him and think of pages of music notes. They bloom black and tangled before my eyes, full of unheard music but beautiful all the same.

ჯ➣ჯ➣ჯ➣ჯ➣

My mother tells me to not be like Shelly and instead find a nice boy, preferably someone who can carry a tune, and stick with him. Also, not to get pregnant. Mom worries that Shelly might end up pregnant, maybe sooner than later, or for all we know she might be knocked up even as we speak. I hear my mother say this on the phone to her sister, who lives in Wisconsin and never played a musical note in her life. So Shelly might end up in a situation someday, my mother predicts over the phone, and it probably will not involve Shelly raising the child in a three-bedroom colonial and teaching her the clarinet.

I should be grateful for our own three-bedroom colonial because my mother spent years living in a studio apartment in a bad part of Philadelphia when she was young. She ate noodles every night and had bars on her windows and neighbors pounded on the walls when she practiced. Then she made it into the Philadelphia Orchestra, playing the very instrument I use today. She was happier in those days, I suppose, until she quit the orchestra and moved into a big house so she could have a husband and daughters.

This house is too large for only my mother and me. My father moved away with his new wife. They have a set of baby twins I want to visit, but I'm not allowed. With him gone and with Shelly away at college, this house feels huge and empty. I fill it with the distinctive and rich timbre of the clarinet.

My mother comes into my room tonight as I practice and watches me intently, as if wishing she could transfer the clarinet into her own hands. I lower the mouthpiece and wait, thinking she might ask to play for a few minutes and remember what it feels like. One day last year I came home and heard her playing the clarinet in her bedroom. I stood at the bottom of the stairs and listened for a long time, and when the music stopped I went outside and came back in again, letting her think I hadn't heard her at all. She was downstairs smiling when I stepped inside the second time, and she said maybe we could order pizza for dinner. She never orders pizza, so I should have been excited, but I could only think: I want to be as good as you.

She looks around my room for a moment, at the bedspread splattered with roses, the lilac walls, the horse posters I haven't yet been brave enough to replace with pictures of famous boys. I hold the clarinet and wait, wondering if she uses sheet music or if the notes come from inside her, invisible and complicated but fully formed.

Instead of reaching for the clarinet, my mother rests her hand on the doorknob and says that I am well on the way to becoming just like her. Then she tells me to start again from the beginning because audition day is almost here. This is important, she tells me, you need to be prepared.

ᘏᘏᘏᘏᘏ

The college sends a notice to our address that Shelly is failing half her classes. My mother, probably through force of will, finally gets Shelly on the phone and yells and yells. It is just like the old days, when Shelly wouldn't practice and threatened to put the clarinet on the railroad tracks and let the daily to Chicago run its course.

Among other things, my mom tells Shelly to stop hanging around with whatever horrible friends she's made, not to mention those sleazy boys, and for god's sake buckle down.

Shelly always had a lot of friends, even after she quit concert band and wasn't in any extracurricular activities at all. When

I was younger, I had the crazy idea that I could join both the baton squad and band when I reached middle school. I know better now. The baton twirlers have hair ribbons, sleepovers, and matching white tennis shoes, and they don't associate with me.

My mother has no idea I want to be on the baton squad. There's a lot she doesn't know about me, like the fact that I really watch MTV and only switch over to PBS when I hear her coming. Or that I stash copies of *Seventeen* under my bed so I can learn what colors go with my skin tone or how to get the baton squad girls to talk to me. Or that sometimes I tempt myself to mess up the audition and let Tameka win first chair.

She doesn't know that I have started to write Shelly secret letters, either. I write things like: How many boys did you have to kiss before you got it right? Is *Seventeen* the reliable source I think it is? If you were quitting band and had to join another activity, would you choose (a) volleyball, (b) drama club, or (c) ballet?

The longer Shelly goes without responding, the bolder I become: Where do you go late at night when you're not in your dorm room? Do you hate Mom? How could you have held her clarinet out the window and threatened to let go? That instrument is worth something, you know.

On the morning of my birthday, I come downstairs to see twice as many presents as I normally get. This is because when Shelly has her birthday next month, there won't be any presents for her at all. Maybe not for Christmas, either, depending on whether the college lets her return for the spring semester. I also learn that these gifts are a reward, in advance, for when I win the audition tomorrow in band.

At first I'm happy about the presents, but then I start opening them. Two new clarinet practice books, filled thickly with notes that look too hard for me to play. New reeds. A gift certificate to the music store. Season passes for the orchestra, which probably cost way more than a pair of designer jeans. A white sweatshirt emblazoned with a clarinet surrounded by swirls of sheet music. I immediately begin plotting ways to avoid wearing it to school.

I had asked for a tall tube of lip gloss and anything from the store that sells plastic earrings and colorful, slippery scarves. The closest my mother gets is the gift of a narrow nylon belt, the kind that was popular two years ago. The jewelry box looks promising, but when I open the gold lid I see a clarinet pin, complete down to every detail like the number of keys and a teeny tiny ligature.

My mother stands smiling at me the entire time I open the presents. As soon as I'm done she goes into the laundry room, still smiling, and starts bleaching a pile of laundry. Then she calls Shelly's cell phone and kicks the wall hard when no one picks up.

〜〜〜〜〜

Audition day. Tameka is already in the band room when I arrive, studying the selection we'll play for the director. She must want first chair more than ever, but sometimes she screws up during the audition because we have to play in front of the entire band and are ranked immediately. That's a lot of pressure for some people, but not for me. I always do my best when the stage is quiet and the director is right there, judging me. If I ever mess up it's during a performance, but then my playing blends in with everyone else and no one seems to notice. But this year the first chair clarinetist will have a solo during the big spring concert, so finally the rich and distinctive timbre of the instrument will get the recognition it deserves.

I know about the solo because the director told me about it in private. Even he assumes that I'll be the one playing it.

Before we get started, he reminds us that our school district has one of the most accomplished music departments around, and that everyone expects a high level out of even us, the sixth through eighth graders. Last year when he said that he smiled at me because I was still a fifth grader, the prodigy, but this year I am normal like everyone else. My mother has already asked him if I can be moved up to the high school band early, but he said they only do that for percussion or brass players. My mom pursed her lips and that night mentioned sending me to a special performing-arts high school. She went on about it until I screamed and she said, Lord you remind me of Shelly right now.

Each clarinetist plays one by one, starting at the end and working in my direction until it's Tameka's turn. To my surprise she hits every note. She's a little slow when the sheet music reads *allegro*, but it could have been worse.

There is a pause before I start. As the last to play I have an advantage, though I'm not sure losing is a possibility. After all, I am expected to win this first chair and the next one, and so on until I'm a ninth grader trying to beat out all the seniors. It will keep going like this until I have an audition for Juilliard, which, let's be realistic, my mother has probably already set up.

The director is waiting for me and Tameka taps her foot a little, either in impatience or to throw off my rhythm. I bring the mouthpiece to my lips and remember to breathe from the diaphragm and form my mouth in the embouchure my mother taught me.

Sometimes when I play, I lose time. It's hard to explain, but I compare it to reading a page in a book and later realizing you have no idea what you just read. Like everything went in and was processed but then disappeared to a place you'll never get to. This is what happens to me during my audition, and as the last note fades away I have no memory of how I played.

I look up to find the entire band ensemble watching me. The director is giving me a strange look, like he can't puzzle me out. I turn to my left to see Tameka sitting with her arms crossed, glaring at the music stand we share.

The director finally clears his throat. He smiles, just barely, and taps the air with his baton and it's all over, and I still have first chair.

❧❧❧❧

Other band members leave their instruments in their lockers or in the band room at the end of the day, but I always bring the clarinet home so I can practice. I'm also not sure I want to leave it alone overnight in school, where lockers are occasionally vandalized.

I take the school bus to my neighborhood and get off to walk the two blocks to my house. When I step into our driveway

Shelly's car is there, the maroon hatchback with the entire back end covered in bumper stickers. I pause, the clarinet case heavy in my hand. My mother used to tell me I was lucky to have a big sister to guide me through life, but as Shelly got older, she stopped saying that. Some of my recent memories of Shelly involve her shutting her bedroom door in my face and taping cigarette packs to the underside of the toilet tank.

When I go inside, Shelly is standing by the kitchen sink looking pretty normal. I can't see any tattoos, her hair isn't green, and she doesn't look like she's on drugs, though you'd never know that by listening to my mother.

The only difference is she seems tired. The skin under her eyes is kind of blue, and she's not wearing makeup like she did all the time in high school. Her blond hair has been sheared into a crooked, ear-length cut. She wears a zip-up sweatshirt that has paled to a purplish gray and jeans that fray around her ankles.

Shelly glances down at the case in my hand and says, I see you're still doing whatever Mom tells you to.

I don't quite know what to say to that, so I ask her what she's doing here when she should be at college. Winter break isn't for a few weeks.

Shelly shrugs. No point in taking finals, she says.

I ask if she got my letters.

No one writes letters anymore, she tells me. Christ, when will you learn?

Our mother walks in from the laundry room. She has a tight expression and looks only at me, not at Shelly. Well, she says. Did you win?

Yes, I say. I'm still first chair.

Well isn't that fan-tastic, Shelly says. She pulls a cigarette and a lighter from the sweatshirt pocket and lights up, right there in our house.

Don't talk like that, my mother says sharply. She reaches for the clarinet case and takes it from me, placing it on the counter and covering it with her hands as if to protect it. This means something, she says. First chair means something to her.

To you, Shelly says.

Yes, to me, our mother replies. But to her, too. This clarinet is worth something. It represents quality, durability, and pureness of sound.

Listen to yourself, Shelly says.

I played in the Philadelphia Orchestra, my mother reminds her.

Shelly looks out the window. You know Mother, she says, most people couldn't give two shits.

Our mother reaches forward and opens the case, as if to prove a point. She gazes down at the blue velvet, the disassembled pieces of clarinet. I hope she notices how well I take care of it. After every practice, I pull a cleaning swab through each of the segments to wipe out the spit. I apply cork grease as needed. If one of the pads sticks or comes loose, I get out the tiny vial of glue and the little plastic bag of new pads and make a replacement. Finally, I take the fine, silky cloth that has been in the case since my mother's childhood and use it to wipe down the entire instrument. It feels good, to take care of her clarinet.

Shelly says, that thing is a piece of junk, and the women in this household should no longer be subjected to it.

No one is forcing anyone, my mother says, looking at me. She likes it. She's good.

Really, Shelly says. She steps forward to the clarinet case and leans in close, examining it. She takes another drag on the cigarette and blows a steady stream of smoke right over the instrument. Then she flicks some ash into the case and pulls the lighter from her pocket again.

What do you think you're doing, my mother says. Put that down.

Shelly clicks the lighter and a flame appears. Then stop me, she demands. She looks at me when she says this.

You're crazy, our mother says. You couldn't set fire to it with a lighter, anyway. You're being stupid.

Shelly keeps staring at me. She's smiling, and the flame is bright in her hand. She's waiting for me to push the clarinet out of reach, to blow away the traces of smoke before the velvet stains, to carry the clarinet lovingly to my room and start to practice.

Stop me, she says again. Just try it.

I look at Shelly, at her crooked haircut and the blue skin under her eyes. No, I say.

She stops smiling. What?

I nod to the clarinet. Go ahead, I tell her. No one's stopping you.

Shelly's hand hovers over the open case, the flame flickering in her fingers.

What are you waiting for, I say. Get on with it.

My mother raises her hand to her mouth, but beyond that, she does nothing. This is the instrument of her childhood, the clarinet she played throughout school and eventually in the Philadelphia Orchestra, and still she won't intervene.

Shelly frowns. After another moment she clicks off the lighter and steps back, glaring at me.

I thought so, I say, and shake my head to show I'm disappointed in them both. I walk up to the counter and close the clarinet case, snapping shut the two silver locks. I pull it off the counter and take it up to my room, where I will clean off the cigarette ash and wave away the remnants of smoke.

Then I will practice, as I do every day. I will play until I lose time, until I close my eyes and let the notes come as if they are being channeled through me. I will do exactly what I've been doing for the last three years, ever since my mother first handed me her clarinet. When I finish, I'll open my eyes to that black body and start taking it apart. I will hold every piece in my hand and feel the weight, bearing it as my own before slipping it into velvet.

The Ballad Solemn
of Lady Malena

From his seat in the front row, he watched Annabelle glide by on the ice. She assumed a focused, competitive expression, her hair pulled into a stiff bun. It was only a practice session, but she still had to look the part to convince the judges, media, and other skaters that she was there to win. Not that she needed to do much convincing. All she had to do was skate with her usual brilliance and the gold medal would be draped over her neck. It would shine like her hair, which he pictured soft and full and slightly curled when she let it down.

So far he had only seen her hair down on the personal interest segments they showed during televised competitions. Annabelle was videotaped in soft blue sweaters with her hair falling around her face. She laughed and told stories about her life. Once they even showed her bedroom, the piles of stuffed animals floating atop a lilac-colored bedspread.

She was fifteen years old. Fifteen years old, and she was going to win this whole goddamned competition, with him right there watching.

On the ice, she lifted into a triple loop. Clean. He clapped along with the other fans. He had watched Annabelle closely over the last 14 months as she progressed from a skinny little girl to a teenager with just a hint of hips and chest. The changes were enough to risk throwing off her jumps, but she only got better, tougher. She was finally old enough to go to the world championships if she skated well here, which was almost a given. She was young but good. So good.

He left the stands after practice and waited off to the side. He wished he could smoke a cigarette. The crowd shifted around him, a mix of star-struck teenage girls and middle-aged women doused in fur and perfume. Even those rooting for the defending champion—a taller, less elegant skater who had the habit of pursing her lips mid-spiral—acknowledged that Annabelle's artistry and consistency gave her the edge.

The first skaters exited and the crowd pushed forward. Fans waved programs and t-shirts and photographs, all for the signing. He knew that a good majority of them were clamoring for Annabelle's signature.

Annabelle. She appeared still in her skating practice dress, a simple black number with two straps crossed seductively in the back, showing her pale skin. Not a blemish anywhere, not even a freckle. She smiled and took programs and photographs from the crowd, her wrist making the same little flourish at the end of each signature.

He hung back, watching. When she had signed the last program he stepped back into the folds of the crowd, making himself invisible.

The official skaters' hotel was somewhat more luxurious than what he would have chosen for himself, but he had already spent so much money on the ticket package and the flight to Boston that paying for a room in this hotel wasn't that big of a jump. He'd waited for Annabelle in the lobby before practice, but she never showed up. He wondered if the hotel staff had been instructed to escort the more famous skaters in through a secret entrance, out of sight and safe.

His luck came the next morning, early, in the breakfast room. Annabelle's practice group wasn't scheduled to take the ice until later that day and he imagined her sleeping in, cuddled under the sheets in her soft hotel bed. Or maybe she was on her back on the floor doing crunches in nothing but a sports bra. But to his surprise she was right there in the breakfast area, holding down the hot water tap to make a cup of tea. She was alone.

He paused, hovering in the doorway. Her parents or coach could be along at any minute. They were crazy for leaving her alone for even a second, that was for sure. He watched as she chose a seat in the center of the room. The surrounding tables were empty, and only a few other people sat over oatmeal and juice in the corners.

He took a breath and stepped forward, getting into character as he crossed the room.

"Annabelle? Hello!" He thrust his hand out at her. "Brian McPherson, with the *Tribune*. Hell of a practice session you had yesterday. How're you feeling this morning?"

Annabelle looked at him, either bewildered or a little annoyed that he had the nerve to bother her so early in the morning. Just when he was starting to think he had made a mistake by being so bold, she reached out to accept the handshake.

Her fingers were cold. She wore a soft pink sweater that looked like angora. Her hair was swept back into a neat ponytail, and at that moment she reached up with both hands to check its tightness, causing the sweater's fabric to pull slightly at her breasts. Good God.

"Nice to meet you," she said, "but all interview requests go through my coach."

"Ah, Grace," he said, waving his hand. "Yes, we've been in touch on and off all week. She told me this morning might be the best time to catch you." He smiled and pulled up a chair. "She always comes through for me."

"Oh," Annabelle said. "Well, I only have about ten minutes before I meet my parents. So it will have to be short."

Bless her heart. She hadn't even thought to ask which *Tribune* he worked for. "Ten minutes is perfect," he said, reaching for his bag. He pulled out a yellow lined legal pad and a blue felt-tipped pen. This was going better than he had hoped. It was even kind of fun.

"I saw you yesterday," she said. "At the practice session. You weren't sitting where the press usually sits."

He uncapped the pen. "No," he admitted. "I never do. I like

to sit where everyone else does and blend in with the audience. To get a better perspective." He shrugged. "My boss feels it gives me a jump on the competition."

She looked confused. "The competition?"

He smiled at her. "The other journalists, of course," he said. He leaned forward close enough to smell her. "You're not the only one with competition, you know."

She laughed a little. "I guess not."

"Now, Miss Annabelle, if we could get started, I'd kindly appreciate it. I'm not even going to ask why you noticed a boring reporter sitting in the stands." Oh Lord, she blushed. She blushed! He couldn't be imagining it.

"Okay," she said. "Ask away."

He paused for a moment, making her wait. The key was to get her interested in him, to feel as if she should be the one making the conquest. "First, what is your absolute *least* favorite part of this whole skating gig? The thing you hate the most?"

She looked up, startled. "What do you mean?"

He took the opportunity to lean forward again. "Come on, Annabelle," he said. "I've been covering this sport for a long time. I know what it's like: controlling coaches, demanding parents, constantly fighting for your goal weight, never seeing your friends, dropping out of school. I've seen it all, Annabelle, and I know it's not an easy life. What you do is ten times harder than what most adults have to deal with on a day-to-day basis." He leaned back.

Annabelle removed the tea bag from her mug. "Well," she said slowly. "I can't have sugar." She looked from the tea to him. "That's why I drink this apple-cinnamon tea. Because it tastes sweet. Is that the kind of thing you mean?"

"Come on, Annabelle." He put his pen down and crossed his arms. "There has to be something else."

She gave him a long look, and for the first time he could see that her eyes weren't really blue but more of a soft violet-gray. "You're not like the others," she said.

"What are they like?"

"They all ask the same things. What's my schedule like, how I keep up with my homework, if I have a boyfriend. They always ask that one—if I have a boyfriend."

He picked up his pen again. "Now why would they go and ask a thing like that?"

She blushed again. Twice within five minutes.

"I'm waiting, Annabelle. What's your least favorite thing? Come on. I know it's not really being deprived of sugar."

She stared over his shoulder for a moment. "I don't think I should say. It would get me in trouble."

"What if I promised you I wouldn't print it?"

She laughed. "Yeah, right. You're a reporter."

He held up his hands. "Do you see a tape recorder? And imagine the trouble I'll get in when you have Grace call up my boss and insist that I made up this whole conversation. I'll have no tape to back me up." He pushed the notepad closer to her. "And here, I won't even take notes. Now tell me. What's your least favorite part?"

She narrowed her eyes. "I don't know what you're up to," she said, "but fine. As much as I love skating, I hate how the figure skating world makes all of us out to be little princesses. It's ridiculous."

"You're saying you don't fit that mold?"

"What I mean is that they ignore your personality and force you to be as polite and boring as possible. It's totally unrealistic."

He reached forward and tapped his finger against her wrist. "But you seem like a nice, polite girl."

"You know what I mean. I'm not supposed to swear or get angry or overconfident or upset if I fall. I'm supposed to be perfect."

"And you're not?"

She shook her head. "Only by default. Because I have no choice. But sometimes I think if I weren't a skater, if I could be normal, things would be different."

"How so?"

"I'd go out with my friends more. Maybe go to parties, get in trouble. Who knows?"

"So what you're saying is you'd like to experiment, like any other teenager?"

She looked at him. "Maybe." She took a sip of tea.

"But the fact is that you are a skater, Annabelle, and one of the best in the country at that."

She wrapped her hands around the mug. "That's right," she said. "I'm here to win. I need to go to Worlds and have a good showing there, and keep moving up until it's the Olympics." She smiled. "Everyone wants the Olympics, but I really think I have a shot. You know?"

He smiled back at her. "Yes, Annabelle. Everyone knows. You're the best skater I've seen in years, and I've been at this for a long time, as I said. In fact," here he paused again, hoping he could pull it off, "I remember years ago, when Michelle Kwan was first coming onto the scene, when she was what—twelve-years old? She and I had a chat in another hotel dining room, just like this." He tilted his head and looked at Annabelle. "I see a lot of her in you. And I can safely say I've never told another skater that before, never in my entire career."

Annabelle turned her face to her shoulder as if trying to hide a smile. He made a show of looking at his watch. "I better hurry up and ask some real questions, Belle," he said. "Looks like it's almost time for you to catch up with your parents."

"Well," she admitted, "I'm not really meeting them for another half hour."

"Oh," he said. "Then maybe we should go somewhere more private."

⚜⚜⚜⚜⚜

He ushered her around the corner into the dim, deserted lounge and led her to a set of plush loveseats arranged in a semi-circle in the corner. He sat on one and she sat across from him on the other.

To help her relax, he asked a series of unremarkable questions: How many hours a day she spent training, her off-ice workout routine, her best subject in school, her favorite bands and movies. He scribbled dutifully in his notebook while she gave her responses, and when she finally seemed comfortable, he tried again.

"Tomorrow's the night," he pointed out. "You could be a day away from becoming national champion."

"I know," she said. "I can't wait."

He tapped the pen against the notepad. "And if you do win, Annabelle? I would say *when* you win, but I'll spare you the extra pressure. If you win, how will you celebrate?"

"There's a party afterward, of course," she said. "Everyone will be there. I went last year, when I won the silver. It was fun."

"And your parents?"

"They'll be there, too. I guess we'll spend a few hours at the party and then get some sleep. I have an exhibition on Sunday."

"Yes, the exhibition." He doodled on the pad. "But if you win, I'd think you'd want to have a little fun." He peered at her. "Do you? Want to have a little fun?"

"Of course. God, if I won, I'd want to really celebrate, you know? But it's not like that's possible. Everyone in this hotel—everyone in town, thanks to the media—knows who I am and that I'm only fifteen. It's not like I can sneak into a bar."

"No, of course not." He pretended to think for a minute. "But I'm an adult. I could help you out."

She turned red again. He realized that her delicate complexion allowed every emotion she felt to shine through. She straightened up a little on the loveseat and looked at him. "How old are you, anyway?"

He shook his head. "Old enough to know better." He slapped the notepad down on the seat next to him. "It's not about that, Annabelle. I want to help you. I've been at this for years, interviewing young athletes like you. They all work so hard and do everything that is asked of them, but they never catch a break. They never get to have any fun of their own and frankly, I think that's unfair." He could tell he had her attention. "So I want to help. Stop by my room tomorrow night after you make an appearance at that party. I'll see what I can do to sneak you out and show you a good time, for once in your life. You deserve it."

She shifted on the seat. "I don't know."

"We could make a deal," he continued. "Only if you win. If you win, then you'll know that you deserve to have a little break.

You've done everything anyone has asked of you, Belle. If you win, I think you should be able to explore that wild side a bit. You're only young once, right?"

She nodded. Glorious God in the heavens, she nodded. He reached for the notepad one last time and tore off the bottom third of a page. He wrote "Brian McPherson" and below that, "Room 406." In one smooth motion he stood and sat next to her on the other loveseat, handing her the scrap of paper. Keep it light, he told himself. Never mind that her body was right there, that he could reach out and put a palm on her thigh or slide his hands up over that soft sweater to feel the rise in her chest.

"Remember, now," he said. "Only if you win."

She took the paper. "All right. Only if." She looked at his handwriting, running her thumb over the room number.

He stood up. "I should let you go on with your day. You must have a lot to do to get ready for tomorrow." He gathered his bag, tucking the notepad and pen deep inside. "I'll be watching you tomorrow night," he added. "Cheering you on."

"Thanks."

He remembered a final moment of professionalism and reached for her hand. As they shook, he smiled at her. "And to answer your question, Annabelle, I'm thirty-five. I've been lucky enough to make my living by talking to champions like you for over a dozen years now."

She nodded and smiled back, and he let her lead the way out of the lounge. It was a testament to how sheltered she was, he decided, that she could believe someone like him had a lengthy career as a journalist. Not to mention she didn't suspect that he had shaved a few years off his age.

No, she hadn't noticed anything at all. That was good. It meant she was already focused on skating a clean long program. It meant she was already planning to win.

On Saturday night he sat in the stands, three rows from the front. Most of the competition had dragged on in an unbelievably slow fashion, but now the final flight of ladies was on the ice for the six-minute warm-up. Annabelle fell on her triple-triple attempt, the crowd groaning as she went down. He tightened his hand on the program. Other girls were too perfect in the warm-up, he decided. It was possible to leave the good stuff out on the practice ice, all those neat jumps disappearing during the actual competition. She had hope yet.

The announcer broke in to end the warm-up session and the skaters stepped gingerly off the ice. He craned his neck to watch Annabelle's progress. "Excuse me," said the woman sitting next to him, her voice as frosted as her hair, her fingers studded with rings. He had leaned too close to this woman's burgeoning fox-fur coat, but it was all for nothing. Annabelle had already been whisked away into privacy until her performance. He had no choice but to wait until she reappeared, bright and tight, on the ice again.

The first skater in the group was of Asian descent, totally flat all around, with a sweet little face and a nonexistent behind, but she was nothing in comparison. She fell on her first jump, the lutz, and from there he stopped watching.

Four skaters to go until Annabelle took the ice. He flipped through the program again, feeling nervous. Did she fall on that triple-triple on purpose? The crowd erupted at the liquid landing of the current skater, jarring him back, and he decided he couldn't watch anymore.

He got up and walked to the concession stand, where he ordered a soft pretzel and put the bread to his mouth but could not chew. That other girl skated clean; he could tell by the crowd. It wasn't right. Annabelle worked so hard for this. Not to mention she was the greatest talent he had ever seen, the greatest skater ever on those smooth white slender legs that came together for the jumps and parted for the landings.

Over the course of the next half hour or so, the crowd continued to scream and clap and shake the arena. The rest of the girls each went clean, one by one by one. Annabelle was in first place after the short program, but that could easily change. With only one fall, she could slip off the podium altogether, forced to stay at home while other girls traveled to Worlds.

It was almost time. He made his way back to his seat, pushing against knees and stumbling over feet in the aisle as the second-to-last skater finished her bows and glided to the Kiss and Cry to receive her scores. Annabelle stepped onto the ice, as sudden and soft as a breeze. He swore he heard the collective intake of the audience's breath. She swirled around a few times and then back-tracked to the boards to take some water and last advice from her coach. She slipped out of her warm-up jacket and he could finally see the full glory of her dress: dark purple with silver trim, a short skirt tapering down her backside. Sleeveless. Silver designs criss-crossed her chest and then faded along her sides.

The scores for the previous skater came at last. They were high, but he ignored that and looked down, waiting for her. The announcer finally boomed out Annabelle's name above the sounds of the cheering crowd. She skated to the center of the ice, that look of concentration on her face.

He leaned forward in his seat, so far that he could smell scented shampoo in the aisle in front of him. Annabelle twisted her arms behind her back in her opening pose, one leg in front and one stretched behind her, the pick digging into the ice. He knew this pose well. A few breathless moments of quiet before the music started, and then she was off.

Her music was something he had never heard before the start of the skating season, the strangely named "The Ballad Solemn of Lady Malena." It was an unbearably sad piece of music that rose and fell in notes capable of either melting the ice or freezing it harder. Throughout those four minutes of chilling tones, Annabelle held the music to her body and then sent it out, soaring, to the crowd. This was what made her special, what convinced him she would be crowned Olympic champion in two short years.

One, two, three clean jumps. The triple-triple combination. The spins, tight and hard, her blond hair caught in that bun. He imagined it falling out and dropping across her shoulders, but it remained as disciplined as her performance, as controlled as her jumps. During the spiral she soared with that leg up, up, up in the air, sweet Jesus, the pull of fabric between her legs.

One last combination, a whammy of a triple-double-double, and then a low swoop into a final set of spins. She ended with a layback position that showcased her dangerous flexibility, and then she crashed her arms in the air to finish with the ballad's final crescendo. He was on his feet; they were all on their feet.

Relief and fear and anticipation struck him in turn as she

took her bows. The crowd stamped and swayed and hollered. They knew she had done it. Little girls called out and waved flags; they tossed teddy bears and long-stemmed roses down onto the ice. Annabelle took her time, waving and blowing kisses. She skated around, picking up flowers and stuffed animals, until she skidded to a stop right by his section. She reached up to receive a bouquet of tulips from two teenage girls who bounced up and down with excitement. Annabelle's little chest heaved beneath her purple dress, those two subtle mounds. She hugged the girls, absorbing their little happy jumps into her own body.

The crowd was screaming, reaching for her. He stumbled forward along with everyone else. She was close enough to touch but he held back, hoping. She noticed him standing there, her eyes star-filled and watching him.

"You did it," he said, as if she didn't know, as if she existed only as a body over a frozen pond, her features caught and hardened under the flashing of thousands of stars.

And then she smiled at him, in her glitzy flirty showgirl way, and held out one long, trembling orange rose from her pile of congratulatory presents. He accepted it, and she pushed back from the boards and skated away. The purple skirt appeared paler now from this distance, dropping lightly against her skin as if even the fabric couldn't believe what it had a hold of, what luminous body it captured in its clinging grasp.

❧❧❧❧❧

After the medal ceremony, he had nothing to do but return to his hotel room and wait. She was at the after party, mingling and mixing, looking grown-up with her hair pulled back. Would she wear the medal there? Did her father step up and put a protective hand on her shoulder when he noticed men looking at his baby? Because surely they were looking. Surely they saw what he did.

In the hotel room he waited with the TV on and his shoes off. A bottle of champagne chilled in the ice bucket, sitting on the bureau next to a line of clean rocks glasses. He sat on the bed, on top of the comforter, and watched reruns of a medical drama. Her life had sparked into focus at last, and surely this fame would present her with other opportunities, other first chances.

Just after 2 A.M., a timid knock brought him to his feet. He crossed the room and opened the door without bothering to look through the peephole first. There she was, standing with her arms linked in front of her. Her hair was down. It rippled across her shoulders, both dark and bright at the same time. She wore a tight black shirt and a tight white skirt—is that what she had worn to the party, or did she change before arriving at his door?

He stuck his head out and peeked down the hallway, first one way, then the other. "Did anyone see you?"

"No."

He swung the door wider and ushered her in before bolting them both inside. "You made good on your promise," he said, turning with a smile. He had to look relaxed, free of expectations. "And congratulations, by the way. Would you like a drink?"

She nodded and turned in a little circle, taking in the room. He walked to his makeshift bar and poured two rum and cokes, wondering exactly what she was looking at. The neatness of the desk? The bedside novel? The single, king-sized bed?

"Let's start with this." He handed her the drink and she

took it, her eyes pooling a darker shade in reflection of the liquid. They clinked glasses and she drank, quickly, taking many small swallows.

"Not bad," she said, and went over to sit on the edge of the bed. "Is that champagne?"

"You could say I had a feeling there might be a celebration in order. Should I open it now?"

She nodded again. The poor thing was nervous, he decided. He pulled the bottle from the ice and wiped off its cold sides against his shirt. He untwisted the metal cap and rested his palm against the cork. She was watching him. Very slowly, he nudged and tugged at the cork, letting it ease back and forth, back and forth. Within moments of his careful finessing, the cork shot up and out, landing on the floor in the hallway leading to the bathroom. A thin line of fizz eased over the bottle's mouth.

He poured champagne into the remaining clean glasses. Annabelle drained the rest of her rum and coke and held her hand out for the champagne. This time they toasted to her gold medal.

"You didn't wear it," he said.

"My parents put it somewhere safe." She took a sip and wiggled her nose a bit at the bubbles. Adorable.

"You've got good parents, Belle," he said. "Most kids your age are the product of divorced families, and here yours are nurturing the career of a skating prodigy. Remarkable."

She laughed. "Yeah, right." She took another sip. "They're miserable. They only stay together in the public eye, like at these competitions. They refuse to be labeled as yet another family torn apart by the sport."

"Well. I'm sorry to hear that." He sat next to her, raised

his glass. "But here's to you and your national title. The first of many, I'm sure."

She looked at him. "Aren't we going out somewhere?"

He lifted his hands. "It's getting kind of late, don't you think? Plus, you're famous now. I'd probably have to smuggle you out of here with a bag over your head. I don't think you'd like that very much."

"No," she said, her tone serious. She took yet another sip and lay back on the bed, a motion based more on exhaustion, he could tell, than anything else. "Can you turn on some music?" she asked. "Something peppy. I need to wake up."

He flipped on the clock radio and found a station playing dance remixes. She perked up a little and sat on her knees on the bed, finishing the modest pour of champagne. She held up the glass and he took it from her, grasping the bottle in his other hand and pouring a more generous portion this time. "Cheers," he said.

"Cheers." And she drank.

It didn't take long before she was laughing with him. They danced around the hotel room in circles, without touching. She challenged him to a contest to see who could spin in circles the longest without either falling or throwing up, and in the end they both collapsed, laughing and gasping, on the bed. He rolled closer to her and pushed a loose strand of hair from her face. "I love seeing your hair down," he said.

"Hmm?" Her eyes bobbed halfway shut and then blinked open again.

He leaned closer and whispered. "Do you know what I'd like right now?" He waited, his fingertips still grazing her hair. "If you ran back to your room and brought back those costumes of yours."

She giggled, the sound fading into the comforter. "You're crazy," she said. "And possibly a creep." She sat up with a bit of difficulty, her hair mussed around her face. He didn't move. She blew a puff of breath at the strands of hair dangling in her face. This made her laugh again.

"Well, why not," she said, pulling herself off the bed. "Costumes coming right up." She headed for the door without even putting on her shoes.

"Don't let anyone see you," he warned. She nodded and hiccuped, which started another round of giggling, and then she let herself out of the room.

He sat back on the bed, breathing deeply. There. He had given her a chance for escape. What she did with it was up to her. He didn't truly believe that she'd sneak back, undetected, with her skating costumes in hand, or that she would put them on one by one and give him a show.

But that's exactly what she did. She returned with the costumes draped over her arm, the garment bags trailing to the floor. He eyed her, evaluating. That she had come back and met his request was a victory for sure.

Annabelle hung the garment bags in the closet and asked which one he wanted to see first: the red dress with sleeves, from her short program; the purple and silver number she skated in for gold; or her exhibition dress, a low-cut black thing with nothing but fringes for the skirt. He told her to try them on in order from short program to long to exhibition, which put the red one first.

She changed in the bathroom behind the closed door, which struck him as both sweet and a little unnecessary. She emerged with red fabric stretched taught over her body. "It feels funny wearing it without tights," she said, and did a few twirls.

"Do a jump for me." He sat down on the bed again and she launched into a single axel, nearly spanning the room. She landed on her right foot and hopped for a moment but held the pose, her left leg extended gracefully behind her. The dress was good—very good—but he was more interested in what was underneath.

She did a few more jumps for him and a sit spin—or as much of a spin as she could muster on carpet—and then hopped back into the bathroom to change into the purple dress she had worn for her gold-winning performance. She emerged a memory of victory.

"Beautiful," he said, and while she strutted around him he reached out to trace the silver lines running across her body. "You look even better up close."

She closed her eyes and raised her loose blond hair above her neck, then let it fall again. She was posing, he realized. Such a show-off. Little tease.

Annabelle disappeared into the bathroom a third time and came out in the black costume, the neckline dipping dangerously close to the tops of her breasts. She'd probably be penalized for wearing that in competition, he thought. She spun around a few more times, breathless.

"Will you do a spiral?" he asked. "That's my favorite move of yours, the spiral. No other girl even comes close."

Annabelle smiled and obliged by extending her left leg straight back in the air behind her and lowering her upper body until her back was parallel with the ground. She leaned out with her arms hovering behind her, palms open and accepting. Even without the speed of ice helping her conquer gravity, she managed to maintain perfect balance. Only when he stepped up next to her did she wobble. She dropped her leg and straightened up again.

"I can't believe you're going to wear this costume tomorrow in front of everyone." He reached out and put his hands on her hips. The fabric felt slippery and dangerous under his fingers.

She peered at him with a bleary expression. "I noticed you right from that first day in practice, when you were sitting in the stands," she said. "I saw how you were looking at me."

"And you liked it." He tightened his grip.

"You're way older than me," she said, but he thought he felt her hips pushed back against his hands.

"You think I'm handsome, don't you?" He ran a hand up her back, pressing her into him. She buried her face in his chest, and he felt her nod. "You want to kiss me," he ventured.

She put her palms against her temples. "I don't know about this. Maybe we should go out somewhere."

"Belle, honey, there's no place to go."

She leaned back against the bureau. "I want a cigarette."

"What?"

"Let me have a cigarette. You must have one."

Of course he did. He had three packs stashed in the bottom of his suitcase. "I don't smoke."

"Give me a break. Just now you were willing to do anything to make me feel good."

"I don't know what you're talking about." He stepped back from her and went to pour himself another drink. "And I don't think you should be smoking."

Annabelle crossed her arms. "I spend most of my time making other people feel good," she said quietly. "So I know your deal. You'll do whatever you can to get what you want. And what *I* want is a cigarette." She paused, thinking. "Or better yet, some pot." She laughed. "That would be great. The skating princess celebrates her first night as a champion by getting high. I love it."

"Annabelle."

"No, really, Brian, you could write about it. Think of the headlines."

"Don't be stupid, Annabelle. You're an athlete. You can't smoke." He had the terrifying image of her holding a cigarette while reaching for something more sinister with her other hand. In those seconds, the vision of her Olympic gold faded to silver to bronze to nothing, just like that.

"You need to leave," he said.

"Don't get all fatherly on me." She stepped closer to him. "I bet you're not even a reporter, are you?"

"Annabelle. You need to walk your sweet ass out that door and go back to your room or I swear to God you'll get what's coming to you."

"And what is coming to me?"

The muscles in his arm twitched. It would be so easy. She wasn't even wearing tights under that costume. He could pull the fabric from her shoulders and push her back onto the bed, lifting her legs in the air. Or if he wanted he could take the time to seduce her with a cigarette, maybe even find some goddamned pot and really get her going.

But for some infuriating reason he could only see her on the ice, stroking around that big cold expanse with "The Ballad Solemn" filling her up. Then the sound disappeared and she was skating alone, without even the company of a spotlight, as if gliding her way through a dim, silent cave.

"I said you need to leave, Annabelle."

She stood there for a moment, her body limp in the black dress, strands of golden hair sticking to her face. Then she turned and gathered her things. She pulled her street clothes on over the costume, slid into her shoes and swung the skating dresses over her arm. "What a waste of time," she said, pulling open the door. "You're pathetic." And then she was gone.

He sat down on the edge of the bed, trying to quiet his heart. It was nearly 4 A.M. When he finally got under the covers he left his clothes on and spent most of the night fitful and distracted, wondering if she had been caught by her parents or coach. Wondering if she found someone willing to share a cigarette. Wondering how he could get the smell of her out of his room.

In the morning he packed his clothes neatly into the suitcase, combed his hair, and left a tip for the maid. On his walk down the hall he stared straight ahead, knowing that if he looked down he would see her on the cover of every newspaper lining the hallway, her whole body humming and healthy with victory. He didn't look down once, not even at the airport or on the plane or during the drive home, where the highways shimmered with the knowledge that a fifteen-year-old girl had just been crowned national champion, the pleasures of an entire country won atop a surface so cold it reflected those who gazed upon it.

To Elizabeth Bishop, with Love

I.

Dear Elizabeth,

I thought of you today for the first time in years. I was in the doctor's waiting room. The woman sitting next to me was called to her appointment, and as she stood up to go, she dropped the magazine she had been reading on the table by my elbow. The moment I saw that yellow-bordered *National Geographic* I thought of you, Elizabeth, and I'm not ashamed to admit it. It was like coming home after spending years away.

I picked up the magazine and flipped through it, thinking of your poem about the waiting room. In that magazine I saw no volcano, no babies with pointed heads wrapped round and round with string, but I was already caught in the *oh* of your voice. And I began to remember.

II.

Everyone these days seems to have a therapist, but since I don't, all I can say is Mrs. Shab would want to know why I'm writing this letter. Mrs. Shab teaches with me at Lincoln Junior High. She wears heavy-duty support hose rolled past her knees and considers algebra God's greatest gift for idle hands. She would not be pleased to learn I am writing to you, even if I lied and told her this was nothing but a bit of amusement to fill my nights. So, in honor of her disapproval, I came up with a list of reasons for writing this letter:

I write to you because you lived in Brazil and I've never been there.

Because you wrote a famous poem about a fish.

Because you once spent a night in a tree.

Because when you were seventeen you walked the length of Cape Cod, from the elbow to the tip.

Because you are my favorite dead poet.

Finally, I write this letter because I once loved poetry and even wrote poems myself, years ago. But that's not the point. My old poetry doesn't have much to do with anything, anymore.

III.

Here's the truth: I write to you because you're a secret.

I don't want to hurt your feelings, Elizabeth Bishop, but the average person today has no idea who you are. And not only my eighth-grade students, who don't seem to know much of anything, or the man who drives the morning bus or that woman in

Armani always on her cell phone in the downtown café. When I say no one knows who you are, I mean no one knows anything about poets, period.

Not that I'm any better. I won't admit this to just anyone, Elizabeth, but I've been known to watch reality TV.

I just realized you don't even know what that is.

IV.

I once heard a recording of you reading your own poetry. I can't remember when this was—I must have been in college, though it could have been earlier than that—and since then I have been unable to read one of those poems without hearing your voice in every word. From lines like *rainbow, rainbow, rainbow!* to the *black, naked women with necks wound round and round with wire,* your voice summons a child who believed in rhythm, in tone. In poetry.

I imagine, in those days you lived in Brazil, that this is the sort of thing you'd think about all day long. Art with a capital *A*. I'm sorry to tell you, Elizabeth, that things have changed. I don't just mean the greater world, with the Internet and DVR and camera phones and that horrible *American Idol.* I mean me. I've changed, and I'm only realizing how much with every word I write to you at this very moment. I haven't even thought of you in years and years until someone happened to slap down a yellow magazine in a waiting room, of all places.

The truth is, I didn't even try to write this letter by hand. I just sat down at my computer and started type-type-typing. What do you think of that?

V.

I still haven't told you why I was at the doctor's office in the first place. Or, for that matter, why I was so shocked to come home and read what *Wikipedia* listed as your cause of death: cerebral hemorrhage. In all the time I spent reading your poetry as a teenager, I never knew how you died. It didn't concern me then.

The doctors continue to assure me that my hemorrhage is mild, and that I have a chance at a complete recovery. (A chance, like the milk bottle toss at a carnival. No one ever knocks down those milk bottles.) What I have is not the same thing that killed you. Not exactly. But it's close.

I should tell you that Wikipedia is an unreliable source, and I meant to double-check that bit about your cerebral hemorrhage. But I never did. Maybe I don't want to know for sure how you died. I definitely don't want it to be linked to me, proof that something serious is going on under my skull.

If I were a poet, I'd come up with some sort of metaphor: the leaking in my brain, the way I've allowed my life to slip away. But the only poet here is on the other side of this letter.

Oh, Elizabeth. I just realized I've numbered the parts of this letter like stanzas. I swear it was an accident. I bet you would never make that mistake. I'm sure you always knew the form of a piece long before you started to give it shape.

VI.

When you've taught one subject for nearly twenty years, as I have with earth science, the honeymoon period is over. I've memorized all my lessons and anticipate the class's questions—if I'm lucky enough to get students who ask questions at all.

You might wonder why I don't teach English. Maybe I was afraid to view poetry as a job, or to spend eternity grading bad term papers. Or maybe I am more drawn to the mysteries of our planet than I care to admit: geology, oceanography, astronomy, the way air and water and rock create our world.

I had dreams like anyone else. I was going to be a musician, Elizabeth. I was going to be a sculptor, I was going to be a poet. I was going to be someone more than a woman who leaves work tired at the end of the day, who watches two hours of television before grading some papers and visiting a few online gardening forums before going to bed.

My story is not a new one. I know this. What's so surprising is to sit down and write you a letter only to realize how *unlike* my own self I have become.

VII.

I was married once. Does that surprise you? The ceremony was a week after our college graduation, and the marriage lasted only two years. I was divorced at twenty-three. You, I notice, had the sense not to marry. Of course, you turned to women for romance, making you free even from men.

My marriage was easy enough to end. By the time everything was finalized it felt as if we'd simply lived through an extended weekend beach party, and suddenly it was time to pack up and go home.

Patrick and I don't speak anymore, but we do send each other Christmas cards. A few years ago he included a note with his card, inviting me to join him and his old college friends on a ski trip in Vermont. It was sweet of him, and innocent, but I declined. We had been so much like children during our marriage that I couldn't stand to travel to Vermont and be reminded of how much like a child he still is.

Patrick doesn't know about my hemorrhage. Not many people do. I guess if I had a choice, I'd keep it even from myself.

VIII.

At the end of the school year, my eighth graders will vote on class superlatives. Most popular, most athletic, most artistic, most likely to succeed. The results won't be much of a surprise—junior high students are nothing if not precise in drawing social lines. The teachers will huddle together in the break room and laugh, imagining where Miss Popular or Mr. Athletic will be in fifteen years. The students who aren't picked for anything will feel abandoned, unremarkable. I was one of those students. I'd like to say that these kids are the ones with the brightest futures, but I'm not much proof of that.

From what I gather about your personal life, Elizabeth, you were never exactly hard up for adventures. You traveled, made a lot of friends who also ended up famous, and left books of poetry and beaming reviews and even a Pulitzer in your wake. No matter what, you kept writing poems and didn't, for example, take a job as an advertising executive to make ends meet and to flesh out a nice 401(k).

I admit it, Elizabeth. I'm bitter. You lived in a time when being a poet was possible. Today, people aren't even reading books. Forget about poetry. It's all Internet and TV and phones that are really computers.

I wish I could stop time and travel back to when you were alive. Maybe you could tell me it's not so bad, dying this way. At the least, I would accept a friendly tea hour at your summer home in Maine, with trees looming in the darkness and your voice— that voice I know so well—telling me everything is marvelous and that the two of us are, after all, the same.

IX.

In one of your poems, you wrote about seeing a moose appear in the road. I loved that poem for being so looming, so *Canadian*. When I returned from the doctor's office today I went straight home and looked for that poem, for the line I had forgotten and needed to see again to believe it was real:

Why, why do we feel (we all feel) this sweet sensation of joy?

I know why, but only briefly. Then the light fades, and I am left with my same old misunderstanding. I am left to my television, my websites, my class of eighth graders studying earth science. And Elizabeth, I am left wanting to see that moose.

I want to witness this animal you described as towering, as high as a church. I would crawl off the bus and leave all the passengers behind—even you, my dear Elizabeth—and reach for the moose and her great antlerless head. I would take my time, grand and otherworldly, and when I turned around again it would be your face peering back at me from the bus window.

You make me remember myself: a young girl sitting on a bus, traveling somewhere, anywhere, with her own reflection hovering in the darkness outside.

X.

That is why I write to you, why I keep repeating your name. And Elizabeth, I am sorry. I'm sorry I forgot about you until today in the waiting room. I'm sorry about the TV and the lazy wasted nights. I'm sorry for giving up on my dreams. For getting divorced, for getting sick. For getting lost. For never seeing that moose.

And I'm sorry for you, too. I'm sorry the world has changed, that poetry doesn't mean the same thing anymore. I'm sorry you had to go and die like all the rest of us will, sooner or later. In the end, Elizabeth, I am so sorry for both of us. And that is just too much for me to bear.

But I'll send this letter anyway, and I'll send it with love. I'll print it out, fold it into thirds, and slip it into an envelope, using my thumb to press down a stamp. I'm not sure yet where to mail it. Maybe Brazil. Maybe to myself. Either way, I won't tell anyone about this letter. I'll keep it between us, saving you as a secret.

I won't even sign my name.

The Second Rule of Yoga

The first rule of yoga is to breathe like you have never breathed before: long, ropey lengths of air pulled past your ribs and through your nose. Do this again, slower if possible, and feel the breath move through your insides. Do this until you go blank or until your body hums, or until you forget and open your mouth and realize you have to start all over again.

The second rule of yoga is to stop thinking. This is both the easiest and the most difficult rule. Lie in the corpse pose and practice the breathing from rule one. Clear the mind. Breathe out every thought. Just when you believe you've succeeded in not thinking, you realize you are thinking more than ever. And worse, you are having the strangest, least useful thoughts of the day. You are thinking: *Ice cube trays take forever to freeze. I need to*

print all my digital photos. Last time I used too much water and the
rice turned out soggy. How can I convince myself I practice yoga for
the spiritual growth, and how many calories did I just burn?

Snap out of it. Focus. Only thirty minutes have passed since
you spread out the yoga mat, and already you have gone through
the main poses and are lying there trying to become thoughtless.
Usually you practice longer, but you had a bad day at work and
came home already hungry for dinner but forced yourself into
yoga. Yoga is not about force or tension or strain; you know this.
In fact, that's rule number three.

The fourth rule of yoga is to eat raw foods. The fifth rule is to
be nice to the jerks in traffic, and the sixth rule is to plant as many
flowers as you pick.

You may have noticed by now that not all the rules of yoga
involve yoga.

The rules that actually concern yoga are: number seven, that
your muscles will shake but after enough practice the shaking will
stop. Rule number eight: no one will believe those arm muscles
came from yoga alone, but you should not be vain and argue oth-
erwise. Rule number nine forbids going to yoga class to check
out other students sweating through their thin tight shirts. The
ancient art of yoga is not meant to stir sexual desires, which you
probably shouldn't have anyway because rule number ten tells you
to be celibate. You are still working on that one.

No, you're not. You're not working on rule number ten at all,
and have no intention to. You therefore also broke rule number elev-
en, which is not to lie to anyone, but especially not to yourself.

But back to the second rule, which is the easiest because it
involves lying motionless in the corpse pose and is the hardest

because you can't for the life of you understand how to stop thinking. While you work on it, your cat circles your head and doesn't understand you can't pet her because you have to lie there and not think. She thinks you're being cruel. Maybe you are. You're also pretty sure that one of the rules of yoga is being kind to animals. You debate whether this warrants abandoning the second rule to sit up and pet her.

No, stay down on the mat. Another ten minutes and you can get up to make dinner. Something easy and indulgent for a good end to your day: maybe pasta, or garlic mashed potatoes. Start with some carrot sticks or celery slices to cover the raw food rule, but later, pour yourself a nice big glass of wine.

That last part would break rule number twelve, which prohibits alcohol. Number twelve is another rule you're not working on, though you can see why it is a good one. But sometimes a beer is a beer and sometimes you like to drink wine while watching movies that are so old the color looks funny. So you give in. At least twice weekly you break this rule giddily, maybe even (do you dare?) drunkenly.

But it's not time for dinner yet, and rule number thirteen is to not fixate on the rules you keep breaking. Instead go back to the second rule, which is to not think. You keep forgetting that one. Breathe in, breathe out. Breathe in. Hold it until it hurts a little. Breathe out.

Rule fourteen encourages you to make sacrifices. Let yourself think for a moment (just one moment can't hurt) to consider the following extremes: Give up sugar entirely. Stop buying paper towels and instead use rags, which can be washed and reused. Donate more money than you spend on yourself. For a moment, feel proud of these thoughts. Then remember you're thinking, and thinking of material things, and sigh out some air and go back to rule number one, the breathing rule, before easing into the second rule. Return to the rule only to fail again. This, at least, is not a surprise.

These rules of yoga amount to a promise. If you do all this, but especially the second rule, you'll obtain what few people ever do. It might be enlightenment or inner peace; whatever it is, you're far from it. It's possible you experienced it briefly in the past, but then you stopped to think about it, and it disappeared.

It might have happened outside, at night, by the edge of the woods with wind in the trees. It might have happened at that camp with the falling stars. You seem to recall it coming when you were a child and the air outside was new with rain. The problem is that these days, you live in a high-rise surrounded by cement and you haven't felt those blissful moments for at least a decade. This is why you're on your back on a yoga mat, trying to find it again.

Your cat makes an impatient noise. Your dinner, whatever it will be, sits uncooked in the cabinets. Breathe in and out one last time and decide you are finished for the day. Roll up the yoga mat and tuck it away. Stretch upward once. Make that stretch last because, finally, here is a stretch without the burden that comes with trying not to think. When you are done stretching, open your eyes and see the sun out the window. Start dinner. Make plans with friends. Eat cookies and drink wine and pet the cat.

Tell yourself today was not your day. Tell yourself it will happen another time, after more practice. Because if you try hard enough or not-try hard enough, this blessed event of not thinking will eventually happen to you. Think of the word *blessed,* the word *bliss.* Think these thoughts until they become you. Think them until they become smaller and smaller specks of dust. Think them until they turn to light, to a release in your chest.

Think them until they become nothing at all.

Festival of the Dove

Jeremy taught his sister to dive at the community pool, where they spread orange and yellow towels against lounge chairs and kicked their flip-flops to the ground. Abi was only eight years old. She kept tugging at her hair and made Jeremy count down from ten before she would jump. At first she simply plunged into the water, feet first. It took some time before she was ready for a true dive, her skinny arms held straight out in front of her chest, the way she took one last quick breath like a gasp just before jumping. She became brave before long, slicing deeper into the water, and by midafternoon she was in line for the high dive. She ascended the ladder on tiny feet and hurried to the edge of the board, where she bounced three times and gave Jeremy a wave. Then she dove.

That was the beginning. When Abi grew older and became

the star of every swim meet, Jeremy took credit. When she won college scholarships for her diving, he went around telling everyone he was the one to teach her.

And when, as a college freshman, Abi went with her friends to a quarry and dove straight in and never came up again, Jeremy was responsible for that, too.

⅜⅜⅜⅜⅜

Susannah Martin, MA, LISW, opens the meeting as usual by peeling away tinfoil to display a homemade chocolate dessert. The girls each lean forward to pluck a treat from the foil. Usually they stop after the first one, but Jeremy suspects afterward they go back to their dorm rooms and eat until they cry.

"Let's talk about trust," Susannah says. She pushes the snacks toward the center of the table. She never eats anything, ever. Once Jeremy saw her in the student cafeteria with nothing but a tall glass of water with lime. She fished the lime wedge out before taking a sip.

"For example," Susannah continues, "how can we trust our loved ones to stay here, when others have left us?"

No one answers, and Susannah is left to stare around the table. She's straight out of grad school and looks about as young as the other students, even though she wears collared shirts and glasses looped with a thin silver chain.

Jeremy takes his grief-cycle handout and flips it over. He draws a girl with straight hair and an upturned nose. He gives her long, striped socks and a strappy black wristwatch. The sun goes in the upper left corner and shines a few skinny rays on the girl's hair, her shoulders. In the background he adds some curly tipped lines. These represent water.

He is drawing Abi.

No, he is drawing the girl sitting across from him. Her name is Gretchen, and she's a sophomore. She comes to the group because her father had a heart attack in the attic last summer. Gretchen and her mother didn't discover him up there for almost two days.

"Anyone can go at any second," says a girl named Karen. "The rest of you don't understand, because a sudden death is different from something like cancer. We didn't see it coming."

At this point, almost everyone in the room bristles. Of the eight group members, four have lost family members to cancer, and one to Alzheimer's. Then there is Karen, whose aunt died in a car crash, and Gretchen with her heart-attack father.

And Jeremy, of course. Jeremy and Abi.

"Jeremy knows what I'm talking about," Karen continues. "I bet you never want to swim again, right? I bet you panic anytime your friends say they're going to the lake."

Jeremy shrugs. He hadn't been there, at the quarry, when his sister came up against those rocks. He didn't hear the news until the next morning, when he woke in his dorm room to a ringing phone. As he listened to what happened to Abi, he remembered that in the beginning, she didn't even want to dive. He had been the one to encourage her.

But Jeremy is not afraid of water. What happened to his sister was an accident. She dove into shallow water and hit her head on the rocks.

Jeremy looks at Gretchen. She sits staring at her hands and is probably thinking of her father but Jeremy wonders, does she swim? Does she dive into clear cold water and break through the surface to emerge dripping and wet and alive?

❧❧❧❧

Before she dismisses them, Susannah taps the table with her fingernails. "Don't forget about next Saturday," she says. That is when the Festival of the Dove takes place, where they will meet for a special group session.

As far as Jeremy can tell, no one is looking forward to this. The university's annual peace celebration is meant to be an all-day outdoor party, with bands and costumes and kegs of beer. Susannah, however, has convinced them to congregate near one of the bridges to hold some sort of memorial service.

Jeremy trails behind the others as they leave Hoffman Hall and step into the darkness. He is the only male in the grief group. Susannah says this is because Jeremy has a great capacity to express his feelings to his peers, something she does not commonly observe in young college men. Still, he is the only one.

The girls in front of him break apart and head toward separate bridges. Marchwood University has five pedestrian bridges, each branching toward a different part of campus. When Jeremy steps onto his bridge, he sees Gretchen ahead of him. She lives in the building next to Jeremy's. He knows this because sometimes, on warm afternoons, she spreads a tapestry on the grass in front of the dormitory and reads there, under the full force of the sun.

Jeremy walks a bit faster to catch up to Gretchen. As he focuses on her form he thinks of Abi, and how she stayed so tiny even as a teenager. She was like a bird: quick, small, soft as feather.

Abigail, he says, just to hear her name.

"What?" Gretchen turns around on the path and faces him.

"Oh," he says. "Can I walk back with you?"

Gretchen nods and makes room beside her on the path. She is almost exactly Abi's size, and for a moment in the dark, Jeremy lets himself pretend it's his sister who's beside him.

When they approach the brick steps of the dorm's porch, Gretchen gets out her keys, glancing off into the dark folds of campus.

"You know what I heard?" Gretchen tucks her index finger through the key chain and swings the keys around. "Susannah's only working here because the last counselor had a family emergency and had to leave. Susannah doesn't even have any experience with grief counseling."

"Really." Jeremy wants to reach out and steady Gretchen's hands.

"One time, in our private session, she even admitted that she's never lost anyone in her family," Gretchen continues. "Can you believe that? She has no idea what we are going through."

Jeremy tilts his head at Gretchen. "You look like my sister."

"What?"

"Abi. You look like her."

Gretchen peers at him. "I do?"

"Yes. I don't know why I told you that." He looks off the porch toward his own dorm. "I meant to ask if you'd like to get together after the festival next weekend."

Gretchen stands under the white porch light and gives him a good stare. Her hair is a bit darker than Abi's and streaked with reddish strands.

"No," she says at last. "That is not a good idea at all."

She uses her key to unlock the front door and steps inside, closing the door behind her. Jeremy stands on the brick porch with the white light shining above him. He counts to ten, waiting to see if Gretchen will change her mind and come out again. She doesn't.

Jeremy crosses the porch and walks to his own dorm, which is only a few dozen steps away if he cuts through the grass. If he cuts through the damp dark grass he is almost already there.

❧❧❧❧

At the next session, Jeremy arrives late to hear Karen worrying whether she can ever have sex again. Apparently her dead aunt has nothing better to do than float around and judge Karen's personal life.

"She was raised a good Catholic girl," Karen says. "I can't bring myself to do it if I think she's watching."

Jeremy wonders who Karen has to do it with anyway but decides not to ask.

"Your aunt was once young, too," Susannah says with a smile. "I'm sure she would understand."

"You didn't know my aunt," Karen retorts.

Susannah sighs and looks around the table. She's wearing too much lipstick, but it's a pleasant plum shade that stands out against her skin. "Okay," she says, as if in defeat. "This is our last group before the festival. To get you through the rest of the week, I have another handout."

She passes out single sheets of paper. Jeremy folds his into the shape of a bird. It turns out awkward but there it is, white and shaking in his hands. He glances up to find Gretchen looking at his paper bird. He slides it toward her and she takes it, tucking it into her notebook without looking at him. When Susannah says they can go and the other girls begin gathering their things, Gretchen remains seated with her hands covering her notebook. She holds it down against the table as if to prevent the paper bird inside from taking flight.

This time Gretchen is the one to track him down in the dark outside Hoffman. She comes up beside him and touches his arm.

"You want to go?" she asks.

He says yes. He does not ask where.

ᠵᡝᠵᡝᠵᡝᠵᡝ

Gretchen takes him to the bridge that leads to their dorms and puts her hand on the railing. "If we went one by one to each of the bridges, how long do you think it would take us?"

"Every bridge on campus?" He thinks for a moment. "About twenty minutes, if we ran."

She nods. "So let's run."

Gretchen starts at full speed and he follows, trying to grab her hand but she brushes him away. They race down the curving stone paths, and she swings left toward the next bridge. Jeremy expects her to slow down but she clatters across it and he's right behind her, the planks bouncing back against his feet. This bridge leads to the dining hall and the athletic center, and beyond that is a short field and then a third bridge opening up to administrative buildings and Old Main.

When they reach the Old Main bridge Jeremy wants to take a break, but Gretchen is still running full force and he can do nothing but follow unless he wants to lose her. The fourth bridge offers passage to one of the most crowded areas of campus, with freshman dorms and tall brick classroom buildings and the stone chapel he has never entered.

Once this bridge is behind them, only one remains. This last bridge leads nowhere, but still Gretchen runs. The north bridge is on the edge of campus, in a location so isolated its placement is a mystery. The campus grounds grow darker as they go, the lights spread farther and farther apart. The last light waits in front of the bridge, glowing pale and sad in the night.

When they reach this bridge, Gretchen races to the top and turns to face Jeremy, triumphant. "All five bridges," she says. "I bet no one has done it so fast."

Jeremy joins her on the bridge, where they catch their breath and peer over the edge, trying to make out the stream that moves beneath them.

"Come on," Gretchen says once she can breathe normally again. "Let's go."

They move down into the dark wilds with the branches and the pulsing stream. It is cold, but Gretchen is beside him and they find a rough path beneath their feet. As they walk, Jeremy adjusts to the dark and makes out the black shapes of trees against a deep gray sky. Soon the woods open into the relief of a clearing, where the stream collects into a slick black pool.

Gretchen approaches the water and dips her hand into the

surface as if considering its weight. Then she drops out of her clothes, right there on the shore. Her cardigan comes first, then her pants, then the shirt and bra and underwear. Jeremy starts taking off his own clothes. Somewhere from above, he imagines Abi jumping and falling, landing and not coming up.

Gretchen slips into the pond and then turns back. "Is it okay?" she asks. "Are you afraid of the water?"

Jeremy is not afraid of the water. He splashes in next to her and they stand waist-deep in a pool black enough to conceal their bodies. He moves toward Gretchen and she splashes away, but then she lets him catch her by the wrist and draw her in. They drift, they float, they go under and come up again, breathless and laughing.

She is so small in his arms. Jeremy could take all of her and place her in a cup, if he wanted.

"So," he says. He pushes back her hair with damp fingers. "Will you stay with me after the festival?" He hugs her body against his and feels a beating surge. She is shivery and warm at the same time. Bird-like.

Gretchen looks over his shoulder. "Last year, some girls and I shared a thirty pack, and then we wandered around the whole day in the sun. I bought a necklace, but I lost it. I was that drunk." She pauses. "That was my biggest concern last year. A lost necklace."

"This year will be different," he agrees. This year, Susannah will try to make the dead come alive. Gretchen's father, hunched with heart attack, and Abi poised on a rock, ready to leap. "I could get through the day if I knew I'd be with you afterward," he says. He pictures Gretchen at the festival, a crown of flowers in her hair, far from the bleakness of Hoffman 107.

Gretchen is still in his arms and when she looks down, water drips from her hair onto his chest. "I can't," she says.

"Why?"

"My brother is coming to visit on Saturday." She won't meet his eyes. "He'll be here right after our meeting with Susannah."

"Oh." So she has a brother. Someone in this world can call Gretchen his sister, can drive to Marchwood University to see her. "Why didn't you just tell me that in the first place?"

Gretchen lets out a breath. "You never should have told me that I look like Abi, Jeremy. That's not something I wanted to hear." She untangles herself from him and pushes through the water back to shore.

"Too bad," Jeremy calls out. "Because you look just like her. You even act like her. Running to all the bridges on campus? That's crazy, Gretchen. You're as crazy as she was."

Gretchen scrambles in the dark to find her clothes but is having a hard time. Jeremy considers going over to help but holds back. He stays in the water and feels with his feet for rocks, but the bottom is sandy and smooth.

Jeremy taught Abi to dive, but he never warned her about quarries. He never said, "A day will come. You'll be nineteen. You and your friends will drive out to a quarry, maybe have a beer or two, and then you'll rise up in that perfect form and position yourself to fly. It will be your last dive, and to your friends sitting at a distance your body arcs like a song and meets the water without even parting it. They can't see what you never considered: the rocks on the bottom, the shallowness. How an entire quarry wasn't big enough to hold you."

Gretchen finds her shirt and pulls on the sleeves first. Then she pokes her head through the neck, and by the time Jeremy wades to shore, she is covered and chaste and ready to go home.

The festival starts at noon, which gives Jeremy a few hours before meeting Susannah and the group at the bridge. He wanders across the campus green and mingles with the crowds. He walks by booths promoting reproductive rights, animal rights, gay rights, civil rights. The environmental club passes out bright orange flyers complaining about Marchwood's recycling system, and the campus peace foundation has strung low looping paper rainbows from the trees. The first band starts up as a fraternity lights a grill for veggie burgers. Everywhere he turns, Jeremy sees girls with glittering painted faces and fairy wings.

He finds himself standing in front of a booth selling spider plants. They are fragments of spider plants, just clippings really, and they grow out of Styrofoam cups.

"You want one?" the girl behind the booth asks. She has a nose ring and dark, heavy eyebrows. "Fifty cents. Proceeds go to the Marchwood Arboretum."

"Okay." He hands over a few coins and selects a plant. Then he walks two booths over and picks up a narrow red marker. He draws eyes, a nose, and a curly mouth on the cup, and then holds it at a distance to examine the effect. The spider-plant leaves sprout up as funky, green-and-yellow-striped hair.

Jeremy writes *Abi* on the bottom of the cup in the tiniest text he can manage. There. He takes the plant and heads to the Old

Main bridge, where he sits on a large rock and waits.

Karen appears first with a few of her field-hockey friends trailing behind her. One of them gives Karen a hug.

Susannah comes next, wearing jeans and a sheer white button-down shirt that hangs open at the neck. Her long blond hair is loose and shinier than Jeremy remembered. She smiles at him and holds out her hand. He takes it, and she pulls him up from his seat on the rock. She is surprisingly strong.

The rest of the girls trickle in. They look different here in the sunshine. They wear the hippie skirts and camisoles that are so popular on campus. Only Jeremy knows that on Tuesday nights, these girls turn pale and uncertain under the yellow lights of Hoffman 107.

Gretchen is the last to arrive. She rushes toward them while glancing from her watch to the walkway behind her.

"Sorry," she says. "I'm waiting for my brother. I'll have to leave when he gets here."

"I already told you," Susannah says. "He's welcome to join us this afternoon. There's no need for you to leave early."

Gretchen purses her lips and doesn't say anything. She doesn't look at Jeremy, either.

"Well," one of the other girls says. "Let's get this over with."

Susannah gives her a dark look and then tells everyone to stand in a circle and hold hands. "Come on, now," she says. "We've been through a lot together this semester."

Jeremy stands between Karen and Gretchen, but Susannah breaks into the circle. She separates him from Gretchen and takes his hand.

"Close your eyes," she instructs. "I want you each to think about the person you lost."

Jeremy tries to think of Abi, but the music from the festival is going strong around them. He imagines what they must look like to everyone else.

"Now," Susannah says. "Focus your thoughts on everyone else here, and the losses they have endured. Think of their loved ones and how fortunate we are to have found one another."

Karen makes a snorting sound. Susannah remains level-voiced and calm, but she applies a slight pressure to Jeremy's hand. He makes his fingers go limp in response.

"When I count to three," Susannah says, "I want you to open your eyes and look at one another. Do not speak. Just look at each other and understand we are all going through similar pain. Then you'll each take turns saying something about the person you lost."

She counts to three. They open their eyes. Jeremy stares across the circle at a girl he doesn't even know. She stares back. Their exchange is blank.

Karen drops Jeremy's hand. "This is stupid," she says.

Susannah turns to her. "What?"

"I said," Karen repeats, "that this is stupid. It's hippie crap. Aren't you supposed to be a licensed therapist?"

The circle is quieter now than ever. "I am," Susannah says. "A licensed therapist."

"It sure doesn't seem like it." Karen steps back from the circle. "This is doing nothing but embarrassing us in front of the entire school."

The other girls fidget and gaze off across the campus green.

"Well," Susannah says. "If that's how you feel, maybe you should leave."

"You read my mind." Without even looking back, Karen

turns from the group and walks across the grass, freeing herself just like that.

"And that goes for anyone who agrees with her," Susannah adds. She looks around at the girls and stops at Jeremy. "I can't force anyone to stay. This has to be your decision."

In the silence that follows, the girls glance at each other and shrug. One by one, they drift away. Only Jeremy and Gretchen remain.

"She can be a jerk," Gretchen says to Susannah. "Forget about it."

Susannah shakes her head. "I'm glad your brother is visiting today," she says. "At least you'll be with someone who understands."

For a moment, Jeremy thinks Gretchen's going to hug Susannah. Then her face changes and she breaks into a smile. "It's Sean," she says.

Jeremy turns to see a young man strolling down the walkway. He wears a crisp button-down shirt, and his hair is cut short and neat. He's probably the type of guy who shaves every morning without a nick.

Sean calls out, "Hey, Greta," and she runs over to give him a hug. They stay like that for a moment, hugging in the middle of the Festival of the Dove with all the activity blurring around them. Then they walk away together without looking back. Jeremy watches them go. Sean has a little sister who looks like Abigail, but he does not know this. He has no idea.

Susannah moves a few feet away and sits by herself on the grass. She tucks her legs up and wraps her hands around her knees. Jeremy retrieves his spider plant and walks over to her. He lowers himself onto the ground next to Susannah and holds the plant in front of him, its leaves trembling from the movement.

She glances over. "You're still here."

"I guess so."

She wipes the corner of her eye. "I just wanted to help."

"I know."

Susannah turns her hands up and looks at the emptiness of her palms. "You must think I'm useless."

Jeremy doesn't say anything. Instead he sits on the grass with Susannah, their backs to the bridge, and for a few moments they do not speak. The Festival of the Dove carries on before them. College kids scream and laugh and jump up to reach the paper rainbows strung between the trees.

"Here." Jeremy holds out the plant. "I got this for you."

Susannah takes the plant and raises it to eye level. She examines the goofy face he's drawn in red marker. She traces one of the leaves from its tip to the soil.

"I like it." She laughs. "It's good."

Then she lifts the cup a bit higher and peers at the bottom, at the word *Abi* sketched in miniscule letters. She looks at this for a moment and then lowers the cup again. She cradles the plant in her lap and stares straight ahead.

Jeremy touches Susannah's shoulder, but she sits watching the festival as if she is alone. Her hands are wrapped around the cup. She stays like this, holding the plant against her body, for a very long time.

The Last Halloween

In the days leading up to Halloween that year, my mother decorated our house with figures made out of mottled plastic: a cat
with an arched back, a pumpkin, a witch with her pointy broom.
We made ghosts by pulling tissues over bouncy balls, securing
them with rubber bands, and hanging them from a tree in the
front yard. When my father came home from work the three of
us spent hours carving a pumpkin, spilling seeds across newspaper
and flicking pulp from our wrists in the process.

I didn't know it yet, but that would be the last year I believed
in Halloween. It was the year my best friend and I would walk
deeper into the dark woods toward the pale glow of fire. But at the
time, after our pumpkin was carved and the ghosts hung outside,
I was only thinking of my costume. I was about to debut my first

real costume instead of wearing a hand-me-down or something already in my closet. This year, I would be dressed as Sylvia Plath, the beautiful and tragic poet who committed suicide.

Of course, since Sylvia Plath was a writer and not someone as exotic or identifiable as Medusa or Joan of Arc, the costume wasn't easy. I settled on wearing a long black dress my mother bought for me at a thrift store, and then I pulled my hair back in plastic clips. I frosted my cheeks with white powder to show I was dead and carried a copy of one of Plath's poetry collections. As a final touch, I placed a plastic bell inside a small jar and tied the whole thing around my neck and wore it like jewelry. I hadn't actually read *The Bell Jar*, because my mother and even Mrs. Wente thought ten was too young an age for such a book, but I assumed everyone would get the reference.

When I finished dressing and came down the stairs, my mother clapped and my father stared.

"*Who* are you again?" he asked.

"Sylvia Plath," I said, not yet knowing I would have to repeat this explanation many times throughout the night. "You know, the poet. She killed herself."

"That's right." He paused. "Are you sure you don't want to be a fairy or something?"

"Leave her alone," my mother said. "Her costume shows real imagination."

I shrugged. Her compliment didn't change the fact that, for the first time, she wasn't coming along on trick-or-treat night. My mother was the perfect Halloween chaperone. She expressed interest when Ariel and I showed her our candy, but she also gave us some space. She waited for us at the edge of each lawn and was never pushy or embarrassing or loud.

Ariel's mother, however, would be a disaster.

I was considering how to craft a last-ditch argument to convince my mother to change her mind when the doorbell rang.

"Hello," called Ariel's mother as soon as my father swung the door open. She drew out the *o* for way too long, just one of her many annoying habits. She stuck her head inside and gave me a quick once-over. "Don't you look *interesting*," she said. This was coming from a woman wearing a sweatshirt with a big witch plastered across the front. The broom's bristles glittered, and a speech bubble stretched from the witch's mouth: *Cackly Halloween!*

Ariel pranced in wearing a pink tutu, tights, and ballet slippers. Her long brown hair was pulled back in a bun. She had recently started taking classes at the studio downtown, and she had probably thrown a fit to get her mother to let her wear the slippers outside. Still, I evaluated her costume with disdain. We had agreed to be original this year.

Ariel stared at me. "Remind me. What are you supposed to be?"

I gave her a disappointed look. Ariel was the whole reason I found out about Plath in the first place. We were researching our names at the library. *Genevieve* didn't produce anything promising, but *Ariel* turned up a book of poetry. When I approached the circulation desk with the book in hand, Mrs. Wente raised her eyebrows, and we had a little chat about poets and "adult subject matter" and even death, until she admitted that what I had read was correct: Plath had killed herself.

I took the slim paperback collection home and read every poem that evening. *The Bell Jar* was off limits, but for some reason

I was allowed to read *Ariel*. Maybe my parents assumed poetry inflicted less damage.

They were wrong. *Ariel* was full of strange phrases like *green as eunuchs* and *bright as a Nazi lampshade*. I had no idea what either of those meant, but I liked the tingly feeling they gave me, like I was riding a Ferris wheel or sledding down a big hill.

"I'm Sylvia Plath," I told Ariel. "She wrote that book of poems. You know who I'm talking about."

"Sylvia Plath? That's not really an appropriate costume for you, is it?" Ariel's mother asked.

I frowned. "I thought maybe you named Ariel after the book."

Ariel's mother gave me a puzzled look. "Absolutely not."

"Time to go," my mother interrupted. She pushed us toward the porch and wished us luck. "Have fun, and don't run. You'll trip over your dress," she told me.

My father peeked out from the kitchen and waved. He was holding a bottle of wine. *Pumpkin wine*, they'd jokingly called it when they brought it home from the store last night, but I knew it was the real deal.

Before we left, I paused to admire our jack-o'-lantern. My parents and I spent forever on it, carving the face just so. I'd wanted a pumpkin with a round, surprised mouth instead of the usual toothy grin, so that's what we did. Then I figured he needed some eyebrows to further express his surprise, so we added those, plus a curly pair of ears and even something that looked like a necktie. It was easily the best pumpkin on the block.

"Weird," Ariel said, watching me watch the pumpkin.

"Girls," her mother announced. "It's time." She swept off the porch in what I suppose was meant to be a dramatic fashion. Ariel rolled her eyes. I shook out my pillowcase and hopped off the porch. This was the year I finally graduated from carrying one of those plastic pumpkins because if you were serious about candy, you needed a pillowcase.

"We'll start here, at the old gravedigger's yard," Ariel's mother whispered. She crouched down a little, like it was this great suspenseful moment, but it only made me notice her knee wrap.

I gazed past Ariel's mother and took in the neighborhood instead. Pumpkins flickered on every doorstep, and the streets were already clouded with children swishing along in their costumes. The air smelled like dried leaves and wood smoke. I felt it come then, that terrified thrill of Halloween, of walking outside in the dark and not knowing when something would scare you.

"Let's *go*," Ariel said. She twisted her pillowcase and wrung it like a towel. She hadn't been as excited to abandon the plastic pumpkin in favor of the pillowcase; she relented only after I promised increased candy profits.

We turned toward the first house. Ariel's mother's trick-or-treating style was just as I had feared. She followed us up to the first doorway and stood directly behind us as Ariel reached for the doorbell. The worst part was that she didn't do this for our safety, but because she seemed to want in on the fun.

"Trick or treat," Ariel and I said in polite unison as my neighbor Mrs. McCullen opened the door.

"My," said Mrs. McCullen. "What nice costumes. A ballerina!" She adjusted her eyeglasses to take a better look at me. "And Genevieve, dear. What are you?"

"Sylvia Plath," I said proudly. When all I got was a blank stare,

I realized she expected something more. "She was a poet?" I tried
to explain. "And she killed herself." At Mrs. McCullen's horrified
look, I quickly added, "And she was beautiful. She was married to
Ted Hughes and she rode horses."

"Ah," said Mrs. McCullen. She reached for the bowl of candy
on the hall table and tossed foil packages into our pillowcases. For
all of my creativity and risk taking, I only ended up with a single
miniature peanut butter cup. It wasn't even name brand.

And so it went, from house to house, with people saying *oh
look how pretty a ballerina* and *exactly who are you supposed to be,
dearie?* I eventually abandoned the suicide part altogether and
simply said I was the poet Sylvia Plath. I held up the copy of *Ariel*
for proof, and this seemed to help.

We wound our way through the neighborhood until we reached
Mrs. Wente's house. She lived on a hill at the edge of the develop-
ment, in an old house backed by a smattering of woods. That night,
in the black and eerie glow of Halloween, the trees were horrifying
against the sky: thirsty, searching, greedy. Ariel let me ring the doorbell because I was on closer terms with Mrs. Wente.

When the door swung open, I blinked in surprise. Mrs.
Wente had braided her long graying hair in pigtails that somehow
hovered at the sides of her head. She looked like a geriatric Pippy
Longstocking.

Mrs. Wente looked down her nose at us with her usual air
of authority. "Madame," she said to Ariel, and then she turned to
me. "Ah, Sylvia," she said, "I'm so glad you have arrived." She produced a box that contained large lollipops—the colorful, brightly
swirled kind, full-sized and probably expensive. "I read your latest
poem and must say I am ever so impressed."

Ariel took a lollipop. "Nice hair."

Mrs. Wente held my eyes. "Out of the ash," she recited, "I rise with my red hair." I recognized those lines from the very book I held in my hands. I glanced down at the white cover and tried to remember the next line. Something about eating men in the air. Something crazy, at any rate.

"Thanks for the lollipop," Ariel said. "And I like your decorations." The porch was crisscrossed with cobwebs and spiders.

Mrs. Wente glanced down at her porch. "Oh," she said, suddenly herself again. "My pumpkin's gone."

I looked down. "What do you mean?"

Mrs. Wente shrugged. "It's Halloween," she said, like that was a decent explanation. "My poor pumpkin never makes it through the night."

"We have to go," Ariel said. She tugged on my pillowcase. But when we turned to leave, Mrs. Wente called to us one last time.

"Panzer-man, panzer-man, O You," she said, her voice ringing clear against the night. It was another line from the book. Ariel and I gripped hands and ran.

"What *was* that?" she whispered. Her mother trailed us closely, making disapproving sounds in the back of her throat.

"Never mind her," she told Ariel. "That woman is a few berries short of a pie, if you ask me. Thank goodness this night is almost over."

We walked the short distance to Ariel's house and stepped into the kitchen, where Ariel's mother ordered us to spill our candy on the counter. "I need to check it," she said, waving us away.

Ariel led me into the den, where we sprawled across the floor on our stomachs. I pulled my bell-jar necklace to the side and rolled it against the carpet, listening to the little sounds it made.

"You know what we should do?" Ariel said. "Go over to Bill and Ryan's house."

Bill and Ryan were Ariel's twin cousins. They lived a few doors down in a house set against the woods, just like Mrs. Wente's.

"Maybe not," I said. "Besides, your mom wouldn't let us walk over there by ourselves."

Ariel flipped onto her back and sighed. "They're my cousins," she reminded me. "And they live two minutes away. Sure she would."

Before I could think of another excuse, Ariel got up and skipped into the kitchen. Within a few seconds I heard her mother saying, "Why not?" and Ariel returned, triumphant.

We gave our candy a few longing looks before heading out the back door and into the night again. Ariel and I cut through her neighbors' backyards. The hem of my thrift-store dress dragged in the dew, and I wrapped my arms around my body. As we approached Bill and Ryan's house, the woods opened up to my right, and I shivered. My mother would never allow this, I was sure of that.

We started to approach the back door but heard voices coming from the woods. "They're out back," Ariel said. She grabbed my arm and pulled me toward the dark, hulking trees. Twigs snagged my dress and Ariel's tights. She brushed at her legs and then came to a halt.

"What is that?" she asked. Off in the distance, we could see an orange glow on the ground.

"I don't like this." I hugged myself even tighter. "Let's go."

Ariel ignored me and tromped on through the woods. After a moment of hesitation, I followed. I was too afraid to turn back in the dark and find my way home alone.

We soon heard Bill and Ryan's laughter. They turned when they heard us approaching.

"Come to join the fun?" Ryan asked. He and Bill were both dressed in black clothes with a dappling of dark face paint across their cheeks. No costumes, no masks. They were only two years older than Ariel and me, but already they acted as if they were too old for Halloween.

I looked down and saw groups of still-glowing pumpkins at their feet. Quickly, I scanned the ground until I found the one I was searching for: a fat orb with a round, surprised mouth and a dignified necktie.

"So you're the ones who steal all the pumpkins," Ariel said. "How many did you get?"

"Just about all of them," said Ryan. "It took all night."

"So." Bill nudged one of the pumpkins with his sneaker. "Are you in, or not?"

"Sure," Ariel said lightly, but I tightened my hands into fists.

Ryan picked up one of the jack-o'-lanterns and lugged it a few feet deeper into the woods. I followed the glow of the pumpkin to see that we were standing near the edge of a steep hill that rolled to the bottom and then spread out into the impossible darkness. Ryan lifted the pumpkin high above his head, and with a yell, he tossed it over the drop.

The pumpkin smacked into a tree on the way down and broke apart. The candle went out, and then it was dark again. I wondered how many pumpkin pieces were at the bottom. Was Mrs. Wente's pumpkin already down there? How soon would mine, the one with the curly ears, have its turn?

Bill picked up another jack-o'-lantern and paused to gaze at us. His eyes traveled down Ariel's tutu and her pale pink tights. Then he turned to me, in my black dress with the wet hem, the bell jar necklace dangling against my chest.

"What are you supposed to be?"

"Sylvia Plath." By then it was a nicely rehearsed speech. "She was a poet." I paused before deciding to go on. "She killed herself."

Ryan raised his eyebrows. "Really?" He stepped forward and snatched the copy of *Ariel* from my hands. "And what's this?"

"One of her books." I felt my face getting warm. It had been stupid, to bring that book with me.

Ryan flipped through the pages and read, "Into the red eye, the cauldron of morning." He frowned. I knew that line was from the title poem, the poem I'd read over and over again, in honor of Ariel. That line always creeped me out a little and made me want to hurry and grow up so I could understand it.

"What a stupid costume," Bill said.

Ariel laughed. "I *know*," she said. "Nobody even knew what she was."

Ryan held the book up and looked at me. "Are you obsessed with my cousin or something?"

"What? No."

"Why else would you carry this weird book with you all night long?"

I didn't say anything. I certainly couldn't tell him that I dressed like Sylvia Plath because it reminded me how things could stop being ordinary and become magic. I did it because she fell in love and wrote poems and rode a horse, and then she killed herself and that horse went on living, unknowing.

"Fine," Ryan said. "You don't want to answer?" He closed

the book and walked over to Bill, who was still holding a jack-o'-lantern. Ryan slipped the skinny volume right into the pumpkin's open mouth. I could see the flame brushing against the pages, making them curl.

"Hey." I stepped forward. "That's a library book."

Bill laughed and moved toward the edge of the bank again. In one strong heave, the pumpkin was airborne, streaking through the darkness. It missed the trees and arched straight into the leaves, where it cracked apart but remained glowing. I glanced at Ariel and saw that for once she actually looked worried.

"You'll burn the whole place down," Ariel said. "I'm getting your mom." She turned to go.

Ryan reached out and grabbed her shoulder. "No, you're not." He smiled. "No, I think you're going to go down there and put the candle out yourself."

Ariel started to struggle but Ryan and Bill grabbed her and dragged her toward the bank. Ariel screamed once, but by then they had already picked her up. With a great heave, they shoved her over the side.

Ariel rolled down the bank, her tutu smashing against the ground again and again. Ryan and Bill laughed.

When she finally came to a stop near the broken jack-o'-lantern, Ariel lay still and began to cry. The flame next to her thrived bit by bit, getting stronger and brighter. Ariel shifted and raised herself to her knees. I could tell, even from the distance and in the dark, that her tutu and tights were torn and dirty.

"You want to join your friend?" Bill asked. The clusters of pumpkins flickered behind him. I considered grabbing one and throwing it at him, watching it explode in fire and pulp against his chest. Instead I stood there, not moving, not even calling out to Ariel, and for a long moment I couldn't hear anything but my breath and Ariel rustling in the leaves at the bottom of the hill.

The loud crack of a stick breaking underfoot made us all freeze. Then we heard another crack, and soon we heard branches snapping in a pattern moving toward us through the woods. Bill and Ryan edged backward, glancing at the stolen pumpkins. Ariel had pulled herself to her feet and stood unsteadily in the leaves.

"Who's there?" cried a voice, loose and laughing. Something whizzed by my head and struck a nearby tree. I looked down once it rolled to a stop on the ground: an empty beer can.

Ryan looked from the beer can to me to Bill. "I'm out of here," he said. Before I could react, he and Bill turned toward the house and left me there, alone in the dark. Ariel started to scramble up the bank but she couldn't find her footing in those slender satin slippers.

The voices in the woods came closer. I could make out a few laughs, all male. "Ariel," I hissed. "We have to get out of here."

"It sounds like girls," one of the voices said. "Hey, sweetie. Where are you?" They crashed through the woods, coming a bit closer.

"Ariel," I said, louder now. She hurried up the hillside but just before she reached the top, she slipped on the leaves and skidded down a few feet. I looked around in panic. I couldn't reach to help her up, and I worried if I tried, she'd only pull me down with her.

"Can you hide?" I whispered, but Ariel had started crying again. "Lie down and cover yourself with leaves. They'll be gone soon."

Ariel made a whimpering sound but dutifully lay down and

splashed a few handfuls of leaves over her body. Behind her, the jack-o'-lantern fire grew brighter.

I turned around to see a set of branches parting and a teenager, older and bigger than Ryan or Bill, stumbling into the clearing. He wore ratty jeans and a long-sleeved shirt that had suffered several stains. He blinked at the glowing bunches of pumpkins on the ground. "What's this?" He turned and shouted into the woods behind him. "Mark," he called to the trees. "Get over here."

The friend broke into the clearing. He was bigger, with dark stubble spreading across his face like a rash. He leaned against a tree to steady himself and gazed around, first at me and then at the pumpkins.

"So many candles," he slurred. "Setting the mood, sweetheart?" He grinned, swaying on his feet. The beer can fell to the ground. I heard its contents sloshing, spilling into the leaves.

He took a step closer, and I ran.

I pushed my way through the branches and ran from the clearing, the pumpkins, and Ariel. I made it into the backyard and I knew I should pound on the door and get help, but I kept running. I could go to Ariel's house, get her mother. I could stop at any house on the way and make someone call 911. I could do any of those things, but instead I ran. I wanted to keep running until I was home, where my parents would greet me and wish me a happy Halloween and everything would be normal again. I'd be back in the house with the mother who never would have allowed Ariel and me to walk alone on such a night. She would have prevented us from going into the woods or playing with fire or getting thrown down banks. She would protect me from drunken men and keep my book safe so I could return it to Mrs. Wente. I would keep running until I ran right out of that poem, the one with the red eye, the cauldron of morning that I did not understand.

I made it to my street and rushed past the neighbors' houses. I sprinted by our mailbox and cut through the front yard. I ran under those little tissue ghosts my mother and I had hung together. I ran up our front porch, past the empty spot where our pumpkin should have been, and then I rushed through the front door.

My parents were sitting close together on the living-room couch, their cheeks red and warm. Two wineglasses rested on the tabletop, empty and faintly stained, and before I shut the door and gave myself away, I focused hard on those glasses, their smoothness, and what they once contained.

The door slammed shut behind me. My parents looked up, surprised. I opened my mouth to tell them what happened, that Ariel was still in the woods with the men who were looking for her, with my book that was slowly burning to death. But when I looked at my parents, so warm and entwined, I couldn't say anything at all.

"Genevieve?" My mother pulled herself up from the couch. She could always tell when something was wrong. She knew everything, but her eyes were shiny from that wine.

"My book," I said finally. "It's gone."

I could not explain why that was the first thing I said, and why when my mother came to embrace me and I started to cry it seemed I really was mourning the loss of that book instead of Ariel, who lay shivering under a thin covering of leaves. I could not explain why I cried into my mother's blouse for five whole minutes before pulling back and telling them where they could find Ariel.

She's in the woods, I told my mother, next to a small fire growing larger. The men are looking for her.

That is what I told my mother that Halloween night, but in my head I could only hear *Panzer-man, panzer-man, O You* over and over until the words felt lost to me, as meaningless and silly as a costume or the pile of candy that remained, untasted, in Ariel's kitchen.

In the Backyard

In the backseat of your car drifts an oversized balloon shaped like an eggplant. It gleams purple and shiny and has a big smile on its face, a cap of a green stem at the top. You and your boyfriend saw this balloon in the grocery store and bought it on a whim. Now it's in the car with you during the five-hour drive to Phoenix, but your boyfriend is not. You make this trip alone, the only way it can be made at all.

The invitation for your grandfather's eightieth birthday party came six weeks ago, printed on colored computer paper with little pieces of clip art for decoration. You decided to attend the party even though your father would be there and you'd have to face him at last. *My father has a father,* you remind yourself now, during the drive. It seems important to understand this.

You grow nervous by the time you arrive and park the car in the shade on the street. You're not stupid. The family is in there waiting for you, to witness how this reunion will go. They'll want to see what you look like. How you speak to him. Whether you let him touch you, even if it is just to shake hands.

You walk inside with a big plastic eggplant trailing through the air behind you. *Hello, hello,* you say, and hug your grandfather and kiss your grandmother on the cheek. The house is exactly as you remember it, though you haven't visited since childhood. Your grandmother has kept her rooster figurine collection. The furniture is the same. There, above the television set, sit a dozen framed photographs. Some you recognize. Others show the faces of family members who have matured beyond your recognition.

Your grandfather accepts the eggplant balloon while your grandmother screams with delight. "He hates eggplant," she laughs. "He hates it more than anything. Did you know?"

Of course you did not know. You don't even know this side of the family anymore. Maybe you should have brought your boyfriend after all. He could meet your father and take a good look at what has terrified you for so many years. They could face each other and shake hands, and you will remember you are an adult, grown out of that dependent daughterhood.

Finally, your father sees you and approaches. "Hello," he says formally, his arms held against his sides. You are relieved he is following the rules. At your request, your cousin had instructed him not to hug you. You felt silly making such a demand, but standing here in your grandparents' living room, you are glad you had the foresight to do so. Everyone always said you were such a planner, so responsible and mature. Just like your mother.

A crowd of relatives sweeps through the room, and you have good reason to wander away from your father. For a while you hover near a black-haired woman sitting in an armchair. No one introduces you to her, so you take the initiative.

"You must be Sharon," you say, and offer her your hand. She smiles and you sit across from her. This is your father's new wife. In another sort of family she'd be your stepmother, the replacement for your real one, the one you lost.

Sharon is an occupational therapist, and you marvel that your father will have someone to care for him when he is sick and old. Your mother was mostly alone in the end. She had you, of course: her only child, the girl she'd always wanted and claimed was enough. Before her kidneys failed, you had believed her.

The party moves to the veranda for lunch and drinks. Here you can sit far from your father and busy yourself with bread and salad, eating next to relatives you haven't spoken to in years. You must have had the ridiculous notion that they would be happy to see you, that they missed you, that they longed to see how you turned out. Instead you notice the silence and realize how stupid you have been. They are angry with you for shutting him out, for shedding this family as if you never wished to belong. Maybe they think you have no right to be here, at least not without a full reconciliation, and maybe that is true.

But then you recall a long-ago conversation, one you haven't thought of for years. Your mother took you to church for a private meeting with the pastor when you were thirteen. You dreaded going and resolved against all odds not to cry, a promise you made good on until your mother told the pastor, "I don't think she'll ever talk to him again, ever." The pastor wasn't fazed. "And why should she?" he asked. Simple as that: *Why would she?* Then he let you off the hook for the commandment about honoring thy father and mother. "A parent can lose his right to be honored," the pastor said. He seemed so sure.

After lunch, everyone sits over empty plates until your grandmother hustles people outside for photographs. You're asked to pose in a group of men: cousins, an uncle, grandfather, father. You look off to the side when the camera goes off. You can't help it. You need a way to disconnect, even to show in a photograph that you're not entirely there.

The party's winding down now, the guests starting to leave. You crisscross the living room and say your goodbyes until you reach Sharon and your father. He crosses his arms and says it was good to see you. You think back to when you were fifteen and realized that he couldn't control you anymore. You paid your way through college, marched in a graduation he was not invited to. Every year you throw away his birthday and Christmas cards because the handwriting sends a sort of rash up your neck. You live this way, year after year, ignoring your father. Sometimes you wonder if you imagined him entirely, if he is a villain only you can see.

Sharon steps in and takes your hand; maybe she thinks she's not allowed to hug you, either. "You should visit," she offers. She's so hopeful that you almost love her. You wonder what she sees in him. Has he cried in front of her, does he bring her little gifts? Does he ever wake in the night and reach for her, just to be sure she's there?

This is the moment that dreaded feeling starts to creep up on you, no matter how much you try to push it away. It is your biggest fear, the one you keep secret and far: Maybe he really isn't a monster. Maybe you are making a mistake. Maybe he will die, and you will spend your whole life thinking, I should have forgiven him. I should, I should. But this, too, you push away.

As you prepare to leave, you run into your aunt, whose husband died of a heart attack last year. You did not attend the funeral in part because you knew your father would be there. Something must have changed in you since then, to be able to come here now.

You look at your aunt and remember what it was like after your mother died and everyone was afraid to say her name. "I'm sorry about Jeffrey," you say now. She deserves this, to hear his name in your voice. "How have you managed?" In asking this one question, you're overwhelmed. How *has* she managed, how does anyone ever manage? Tears well up and threaten to slide down your face, the one thing you wanted to avoid today. They are tears for Jeffrey, tears for your mother, tears for the family you have abandoned. You cry for the men: your father, grandfather, the cousins. You cry for the men because you couldn't even see them from the cover of your mother's death.

The aunt is touched by your concern. For one moment you savor what feels like forgiveness. She reaches out to hug you, to accept you. Then she lets you go.

There is nothing left to do but start the long drive home. You pass through the front door and walk toward your car, glancing back once. You know this house and its landscape: the flat stone path leading past the citrus trees, the backyard sprinkled with bird feeders. This is the house you came to as a child, but you are no longer a child. You are a young woman without a mother, without a father.

Now is not the time to think about all this. For now, you will go home. You will sleep. You will wake and tell your boyfriend about the party but keep some parts to yourself, those uncertain secrets. Time will pass until you're centered and solid back in your life.

After about a week, your grandmother calls. With her voice sounding far away, she thanks you for coming. She says everyone was thrilled to see you, and that they all said things like, "Hasn't she turned into a lovely young woman?"

Then she tells you how she and your grandfather left the eggplant balloon tied up in the backyard. It eventually lost some of its air and the wind knocked it against the house again and again. It stayed there for days, battered and brave and defiant, just barely holding on.

A System Based
on Counting

On Saturday morning at the Oh, Charlie! Bagel Company, Tabitha wraps the apron strings twice around her waist, knotting them into a bow at the small of her back. She uncovers the cream-cheese tubs, brews the flavored coffee, and arranges the jars of tea in two even rows. She sweeps the patio and gives the industrial bagel toaster a quick polish. Then she brings the blueberry bagels out from the kitchen and starts counting, every berry in every bagel, as if she has never given it up.

The day goes downhill from there. First she brings the wrong order to the drive-through window and is reprimanded by the customer. Then she drops a full bag of bagels while walking to the window. The top two bagels—pumpernickel—roll out onto the floor. Tabitha freezes, but when she sees that no one has noticed she stuffs them back into the bag.

"Here you go." She holds out the bag and smiles at the driver.

"Oh, lovely," the woman says. "Still warm."

Tabitha watches the woman drive away and thinks of the routine she'll follow at home: sweep the floors twice, scrub the bathroom top to bottom, and bleach every surface. Then she'll search the whole place, and if she finds any bugs she'll strike quickly, without mercy. Just this morning she found a centipede crawling along the floor near her bookcase. She wiped it out with bleach so strong the scent still lingers on her fingers. She lifts her hands to her face now and thinks of that bug. She remembers the way it crawled so confidently across the floor and how she obliterated its whole life, its small idea of home.

When there's a lull in the drive-through line she wanders toward the front of the store. No customers there, either. The other girl is nowhere to be seen, which must mean she's having a smoke out back. Tabitha slides up to the bagel counter and looks at the tubs of cream cheese. Seven kinds—odd numbers are unlucky, but this doesn't stop her. She counts the tubs slowly, relishing the colored cheeses inside. She counts them six times without stopping.

The entrance bells jangle. Tabitha steps away from the cream cheese and looks up to see Ron striding toward the counter.

"Hi, Cupcake," he says. "How about it?"

"Coming right up." She drops a bagel into the toaster. The manager is off so she can stuff Ron full of whatever he wants. Her best friend McKenzie is out of town, so Tabitha is left with only Ron this weekend, which might be okay if he hadn't given her a do-it-yourself electronics book for her birthday. Not to mention that he's wearing the damned pre-ripped baseball hat she hates so much, and he obviously didn't shave that morning. When he doesn't shave he gets the whisper of a mustache, scraggly hairs that remind her of spider legs.

"What?" he asks, leaning toward her. "Hey, Buttercup. What's the matter?"

Tabitha shakes her head. "Nothing," she says, but something has shifted. Before she can stop herself she's counting those hairs on his upper lip. One, two, three, four, five, six, seven, eight. And then again. And again. And again.

This dark urge to count started long ago, but it became worse when she left home for college. Four days until the weekend, she'd say to herself when she was alone in her dorm room. Four days until I get to go home.

Which would have been okay, but then she started counting anything that reminded her of home. The framed photographs on her desk, the old stuffed animals she'd brought and sheepishly tucked into her closet shelves. One, two, three, four, five pictures, she'd count before falling asleep. One, two, three, four stuffed bears.

It progressed to counting all of her possessions before leaving her room. Sometimes this made her late for class, but she did it anyway. Eventually, the pull to count was so strong she did it even when her roommate was there. Tabitha remembers how she stood in the center of the room on that ugly rose-colored carpet and pointed at each of her things while the roommate looked on. At least Karen was a sport about it. She just sat on the bed with her knees pulled up to her chest, watching silently as Tabitha counted.

That didn't last long. None of it: the roommate, the dorm, college. Tabitha returned home but still could not stop counting, and she was miserable until McKenzie came along.

She met McKenzie at a concert, where they discovered they were both big fans of the opening band, Ginkgo Girls. They danced next to each other that night, the sweat and dizzy lights filling Tabitha up. McKenzie bought the new CD and pressed it into Tabitha's hands with a little smile. That was nearly two years ago. Tabitha still reserves a permanent place for the Gingko Girls album in her three-disc stereo, and in fact that's why she still has that ancient piece of Panasonic junk in the first place.

Now McKenzie has the nerve to go home for the weekend to her mother, a woman who once celebrated Christmas with not a tree but a cactus. She put tinsel on there and everything, and a little star for the top but it kept falling off until McKenzie jabbed it through one of the spines. Why McKenzie would leave an unlimited stream of bagels and conversation for even a weekend is a mystery to Tabitha.

Tabitha already can't wait until she can stand outside again on McKenzie's balcony. McKenzie would smoke cigarette after cigarette, flicking ash down to the apartments below, while Tabitha counted the balcony rails. She'd count them slowly, taking her time. If she was careful, McKenzie might not even notice. If Tabitha did everything just right, maybe McKenzie would never ask her to leave. They'd both remain outside, waiting for the wind to cross the city buildings and land in their hair, their mouths.

〰〰〰〰〰

On Sunday she tries to call McKenzie to tell her about the wasp she found buzzing through her living room, but McKenzie doesn't pick up. Tabitha stews over this for a while, and then she grabs a tennis shoe and smacks the wasp against the wall as hard as she can.

"Stupid," she says to the dead wasp. "Pay more attention."

She sweeps the floor two extra times and rolls a bleach sponge between her palms to get the smell. She inhales and feels better instantly. When her phone finally rings it's not McKenzie, or even Ron. It's her mother, and when Tabitha sees the caller ID she recoils.

"I'm not home," she says aloud in her apartment. The phone keeps ringing, and she feels silly. It's a cell phone, so she can't use the excuse of not being home. And she's never *really* home, anyway. Not anymore.

She caves in the middle of the fourth ring. "Hi, Mom. Haven't heard from you in a while."

"It's not my fault you never pick up," her mother says. "Or call back."

"It's just that I'm so busy. You understand."

"Busy doing what? Working at that bagel place? You wouldn't be there for half a second if you had stayed in college."

"You always do this."

Her mother takes a breath. "Fine. I'm sorry. But I want to see you. Let's get together this week. For some tea?" Her mother's voice is small. Tabitha thinks of the ladybug she recently tossed outside, the neatness of its little feet, the hardness of its back. She feels some remorse, now, for discarding it so heartlessly. But what else could she do? This is her home. She must protect it.

"How about tomorrow? I'm off work."

"Good." Her mother sounds relieved. "I'll meet you at Jonathan's, on Fourteenth Street. It's such a nice place. Your father and I . . ." and here she trails off as she tends to when mentioning Tabitha's father. She knows Tabitha would prefer to not speak of the whole business, of how he got up after watching an episode of *60 Minutes* and committed suicide in the garage. As if he'd made a list: Saturday, mow lawn. Sunday, cook hamburgers, watch Mike Wallace, sit in the garage with the car running until everything goes black.

"I've never been there," Tabitha tells her mother, but she knows of the place. A ritzy tearoom with a man's name. It's ludicrous. "I know where it is. I'll see you at one o'clock, okay?"

Tabitha closes her cell phone and lifts a hand to her face, breathing in that bleach smell once more. Tomorrow is Monday. McKenzie said she'd be back on Monday night. Tabitha keeps the cell phone by her side, just in case McKenzie calls. So she can be ready. So she can be there when her friend's name flashes upon the screen, as mysterious and glowing as she is in real life.

✂✂✂✂

That night, late, Tabitha drags her mesh laundry bag downstairs. Living above the building's laundry room means she can hear the machines in her apartment. She likes this. She likes sitting on her couch and listening to that distant hum and sometimes, if she's still enough, she can even feel the vibrations throughout her body. These are the sounds of someone being busy and domestic. It reminds her of growing up in that big house in the suburbs, when noises from the appliances permeated the house in their gentle, expected ways. These are the sounds of a household, of people living together out of love. A family.

Sometimes she starts a load of laundry late at night and then returns to her apartment to fall asleep to the sounds, pretending she is in someone else's home. Usually she'll sleep through until morning, and when she wakes, her clothes are still in the washer, damp and wrinkled and clinging to the sides.

On Sunday night, though, her nap is interrupted by a soft tapping at the door.

"The hell?" she mutters, pulling herself off the couch so she can peer through the peephole. It's Ron's face, distorted and strange. This is her boyfriend standing before a funhouse mirror, his flaws amplified. As if through a haze, Tabitha remembers when she felt nothing but affection for Ron. Once, he had been her best friend. Once, she had been content.

"Buttercup," he says when she lets him in. He smells of fried foods and smoke from his job at the restaurant. "I knew you'd be up. You're such a night owl."

"I've had a long day," she says, irritated that the wash cycle ended. Now there's only silence below her. "And I need to put my clothes in the dryer."

"I'll take care of that," Ron says, giving her a peck on the cheek. "And then when I come back maybe I can relax you a little. Help you sleep." He grins. Tabitha sighs and resigns herself to the fact that he'll want to do it on her bedspread and then lie next to her talking. It exhausts her, the thought of all that movement and sweat. But this is what they do. This is what she must do, what relationships are made of.

When Ron gets back from the laundry room he touches her arm. "It's nice to be alone," he says softly. "Just you and me." He runs his hand down her skin, and she doesn't know how to tell him they aren't alone, that maybe they never were. She imagines all the insects that could be watching them as they move to the bedroom, as Ron lifts the shirt over her head. She closes her eyes and starts counting the spots appearing inside her eyelids, and then the number of times Ron moves against her body. It's a lot to count. The numbers go higher and higher until she gets dizzy and loses track.

Afterward he calls her Cupcake and dabs the sweat from her forehead. He wants to stay the night but she encourages him to leave, explaining that she's meeting her mother for tea the next day.

"That's nice," Ron says. They are stretched out next to each other on the bed, their bodies long and straight and barely touching. "That's good, Tabby. You don't see your mom much anymore." He drops a hand to her stomach and leaves it there, giving her heat.

She and Ron have been dating for about a year, ever since the day he came into Oh, Charlie! and ordered a cup of tea. Now she feels sorry for him. She wonders if, after she leaves him, he'll find out he was never the one she really wanted. Tabitha closes her eyes and thinks of someone darker, someone smoky and rich and swelling with life.

But she doesn't break up with Ron, not that night. He is too much like a child in her apartment, like the girl she once was, counting in a dark dorm room. So she says nothing. She even smiles at him, but her smile comes from this secret knowledge: Once he is gone, her life will be cleaner. She will be closer to building what she always wanted.

At Jonathan's, Tabitha scowls at her scone, at its raisins and little side dish of clotted cream. No bagels and cream cheese here. She glances at her mother. It's been only three months, but her mother looks older, those little lines surrounding her eyes like water spiders.

"This is so nice," her mother says. "So very nice to be out with my wonderful daughter for a cup of tea."

"Wonderful," Tabitha repeats dryly. She's only meeting her mother to set her free. She'll cut her out just as she will cut Ron out. Just as soon as she figures out how.

"Your father would be so happy to know we're here together," her mother says. She reaches for more clotted cream.

Tabitha tenses. "Don't bring him into this," she warns. Her father might be sitting right there with them, sipping some Earl Grey, if it weren't for her mother and her nagging. Without her he might have been happier. Without her he might not have ended it in a garage, of all places.

"Well," her mother says, leaning across the table. "We don't have to talk about Dad. Let's talk about you. Are you still seeing Ron? Have you given more thought to going back to college?"

Always, she slips that last one in there. Tabitha digs her index finger into the scone to pop out a raisin. She just wants to take a nap in her clean, bug-free apartment and wake up alone. It would be so nice, to wake up alone.

"I'm about to dump Ron," she says. "And I'm not going back to school. I still work at Oh, Charlie! and I think I might stay there. Try for management."

Her mother's face falls. "Honey, you know there's no future in that."

"If I need more money," Tabitha continues, "I can get a job cleaning toilets in the high-rise office buildings. You have all night to do it and just go from bathroom to bathroom at your leisure."

Her mother pushes back her decaf green tea and lowers her head to stare at the table. Tabitha looks down, too, and notices the little container of sugar packets. Yellow, pink, and blue. Brown for raw sugar, her favorite. She reaches out and touches one of each color. Before she puts her hand down she reaches over again, touching the colors in the same order. One, two, three, four. One, two, three, four.

Her mother watches her. "Honey," she says quietly. "Oh, Tabitha. You're getting worse."

Tabitha tries to pull her hand away but can't, so she counts the sugars one more time. It's always just one more time. This is what she tells herself to get through it. This is how she lives.

Her mother reaches out and grasps Tabitha's hand and pulls it away from the sugar. "Stop," she says. "We'll have you see Dr. Cohen again. We'll get you back on the medication."

Tabitha wrenches her hand away. "Dr. Cohen is an old bastard," she says. She glances at the sugar packets. Maybe she could count them one more time.

Her mother wipes at her face with a napkin. "I'm trying to help you."

"I'm doing fine on my own." For some reason, the words sound a bit wobbly, but she presses on. "And I won't be doing this again."

"What?"

"This." Tabitha gestures to the tearoom. "Meeting for lunch, or tea, or whatever. I just want to be left alone." Tabitha puts down her napkin and manages a smile. There. That's not so bad. "Goodbye, Gladys."

It's the first time she's called her mother *Gladys*, and it feels right. It feels even better to slide off the stiff-backed chair and wander out of the tearoom, ignoring her mother's pleas for her to stay. She passes all the quaint round tables and the hostess area staffed by a graying man—could this be Jonathan?—and it is under his disapproving gaze that she slips outside. Then she turns left, knowing there has to be one around here somewhere. She passes about a half dozen antique shops and a Starbucks before finally finding what she was searching for: a storefront with the cheerful blue-and-white-striped awning, that familiar haven.

Tabitha goes into the Oh, Charlie! bagel shop and orders a toasted sesame bagel absolutely smothered in cream cheese. It isn't the same store she works at, so she doesn't have to make conversation with the bagel girl, doesn't have to pretend the bagels are awful when really they are delicious, soft and full of fatty spread. This is so much better than a scone. This is so much better than being with her mother.

She finishes her first bagel and goes back to the counter to order another. If she were to show her employee badge she'd get a discount but she doesn't bother. She'd rather no one knew she was connected to this bagel chain so she can just sit in the corner and work the chewy dough between her teeth. She doesn't even bother to wipe the traces of cream cheese from her cheek.

❧❧❧❧

When she gets home she starts cleaning right away. She starts by sweeping the hardwood floors and, as always, comes up with dust. She cleans and cleans and cleans some more, but still there is the dust. What is dust, anyway—flakes of dead skin? So she's cleaning herself up, sweeping millions of little deaths into the trash. Disgusting.

Tabitha goes into the bedroom and sweeps hard into every corner. Even after all this time she still finds bits of kitty litter, though her cat has been dead for months now. Then she goes through the routine of closing her eyes and sweeping frantically under the bed. She only gets another pile of dust, but somehow this is worse. She wonders what she's missed, what she's left behind.

Before she begins on the bathroom she decides to get it over with. She picks up her cell phone—still no call from McKenzie—and dials Ron's number. They've dated long enough for him to deserve a proper breakup, something in person, but instead she tells him over the phone that they are through.

Ron is quiet for a moment, until he finally says, "Are you okay?"

Tabitha ignores this question and prattles on for a minute about how he was such a good boyfriend, really, and he shouldn't have any problems moving on. That blond girl at the restaurant smiles at him every chance she gets, now isn't that right? But Ron doesn't hear any of this and asks, yet again, whether she is okay. And then he asks again. And again, and again, until she hangs up on him. Then she goes into the bathroom and scrubs the sink and toilet furiously, her hands turning pink with the effort.

She's almost done when her cell phone trills to life, the special ring reserved for one person. McKenzie. Tabitha punches at buttons almost blindly until she's connected to her friend.

"I'm back," McKenzie says, and then her breath comes out hard against the phone. She must be smoking a cigarette. "You want to go to the diner?"

"Sure," Tabitha says, and she puts on her jacket and walks out of her apartment all while keeping McKenzie pressed up against her ear. She makes it to their favorite diner in less than fifteen minutes and finds McKenzie already there, waiting in a booth. I knew it, Tabitha thinks with a smile. She missed me, too.

Tabitha slides into the booth and faces her friend. McKenzie looks like her name: sullen, dark, a bit masculine. And beautiful. God, McKenzie is beautiful. She drinks coffee out of a chipped mug, never mind that it's already dark outside, and swings a hank of black hair over her shoulder when it drops into her eyes.

"I thought of you when I was at my mom's," McKenzie says. She's wearing a shirt the color of a rainbow-swirl lollipop, something Tabitha could never pull off. "She bought this new painting and hung it over the couch. Very abstract, full of color. It reminded me of the stuff you used to paint." She stubs out her cigarette. "It was so cool when you painted, Tab. Maybe you should start again."

Tabitha is touched by the compliment. She feels hopeful, sitting in the diner eating soggy fries and squirting ketchup into smiley faces on her plate. Tabitha takes a peek at her friend. McKenzie has these lips that always look puffy from kissing, and her skin somehow stays pale even in the summer.

"What are you looking at?" McKenzie asks. She lights a new cigarette and glares across the countertop. One thing McKenzie does not have is a patient nature.

Tabitha leans back in the booth and shakes her head. This is not the right time. "Sorry," she says. "My mind got away from me there."

ﯽﯽﯽﯽ

Her mother calls as Tabitha is walking home but she ignores the call and counts her steps instead. One, two, three, four. But even the counting won't let her stop thinking of home, of that big house with green shutters she once loved so much. It was her father's home, really. He took such good care of it, and even now when Tabitha smells mulch or paint or grass clippings she thinks of him, of his work.

She eventually falls asleep on the couch—someone must have started a load of laundry downstairs—and when she is startled awake again it's almost noon. Immediately she thinks of McKenzie and how she can finally set things right. Tabitha gets so excited that she calls her right away.

"Hey. Can I come over? I'll bring breakfast."

"If you want," McKenzie says.

Pleased, Tabitha dresses in her favorite jeans and the green sweater that accentuates her breasts. The jeans are a little tight but she doesn't worry about that. She hurries out of her apartment and rushes to the nearest Oh, Charlie! to pick up bagels. She gets a full dozen, all flavors, and also picks up two tubs of plain cream cheese.

McKenzie is watching cartoons when Tabitha comes in, and she barely glances at the bagels.

"You're not hungry?" Tabitha spreads cream cheese onto a blueberry bagel. Which has exactly twenty-seven blueberry chunks. "It's funny, I feel like I'm supposed to like flavored cream cheese, but plain is my favorite. I think I'll only order plain from now on and not bother with anything else."

McKenzie eyes her steadily. "Maybe you should take a break from cream cheese entirely," she suggests.

"What do you mean?"

"Christ, Tab. You're getting fat." McKenzie rolls her eyes and turns back to the television, where a mouse is tormenting a cat with a stick of dynamite hidden in a bag of catnip.

Tabitha looks down at her body. That's a lie. She's exactly the same size as she's always been. Well, it's true she usually hovered between a size eight and ten, and lately it's been closer to the size ten, but still. She finishes her bagel and half of another one while McKenzie continues sitting on the couch, watching the cat and mouse run around and around, never getting anywhere.

"I can't go back to my apartment," she announces at the commercial break, swallowing the last bit of bagel. "Too many bugs."

McKenzie raises her eyebrows and looks at her. "Not this again."

"I'm serious. There are bugs everywhere. I'm constantly cleaning, but they keep showing up."

"No way you have a bug problem," McKenzie says. "You live in a palace compared to this place. Look at it. It's shit."

Tabitha glances around the apartment and silently agrees, but she doesn't see even one bug. "I can't go back," she says, and maybe it will be this simple. She'll stay, and McKenzie will love her.

McKenzie reaches out and snatches the bag of bagels away. "Well, you can't stay here," she says darkly.

Tabitha is still holding the butter knife she was using to spread cream cheese on the bagels. She breathes heavily for a moment and throws it on the floor, never mind that it's still sticky. Then she gets up and straddles McKenzie on the couch.

"I'm not fat," she tells her friend in a clear, loud voice, and then she kisses her. She puts her tongue in McKenzie's mouth and fumbles around, trying to stick her hand up her shirt.

McKenzie puts both of her hands flat against Tabitha's chest and pushes so hard that Tabitha falls backward off the couch and lands on the floor. She looks up at McKenzie, who has scrambled back so she is standing up on the couch. As if Tabitha is a centipede or a spider or a slinky trail of ants.

"Get. Out." McKenzie's voice is shaking. Tabitha has never heard her voice shake before.

Tabitha stands up, still a little shocked from her fall. She walks over to the door and opens it, and she knows when she shuts it again McKenzie will rush over and turn the deadbolt. She considers giving one last glance back but decides against it. She wants McKenzie to remember her as the girl who once made artwork and danced with her at a concert. Not like this.

☙❧☙❧☙❧

By the time she gets back to her apartment, Tabitha realizes McKenzie is right: she needs to do something about her weight.

She's been stupid, working so hard to clean out her apartment but ignoring her body the whole time. All that junk she eats is probably attracting insects and disease.

She walks the thirteen blocks (the unluckiest of numbers, but it can't be helped) to the library and finds some books on fasting. The authors smile crazily at her from the dust jackets, and Tabitha smiles back. Heal yourself with juice, the books suggest. Rid yourself of toxins. Tabitha nods at each of these promises and eventually settles on a variation of a juice fast, which involves making concoctions of lemon juice, pure maple syrup, and cayenne pepper. She won't eat for twelve days, and this will allow her stomach to grow empty and stand shiny and pink in her center. The system is practically based on counting: counting the days, counting the glasses of juice she drinks, counting the tablespoons of ingredients. It is brilliant.

It takes four days for the hunger to go away, and Tabitha is encouraged, never mind the sticky sweetness of the maple syrup. No matter how careful she is, tiny droplets somehow ooze onto the kitchen counter, and later she finds bugs there, greedy ones growing fat from sugar, rolling around in the mess she made to clean her own body. She wipes the bugs out with paper towels drenched in bleach, and the smell is so strong she can't bear it. She runs to the bathroom and vomits into the toilet, and when she finishes she looks down in wonder. She'd felt empty, so clean and pure, but apparently there is still something to come up. She flushes the toilet but stays on the floor, wondering what she is going to do.

She drags herself to the phone and dials Ron's number. He does not pick up. "What am I going to do?" she says into his voicemail. She only hears the silence of a device waiting to record her voice. McKenzie isn't even an option. She won't return Tabitha's calls at all anymore, and already that balcony is growing distant in Tabitha's memory, like an idea of home she once carried around in her pocket.

Tabitha goes to the bookcase and starts counting the books, but this just makes her feel worse. Of course, it always makes her feel worse. With desperation, she dials her mother.

"What am I going to do?" she asks, without even saying hello.

"Tabby," her mother says in that measured, even tone that once infuriated Tabitha but now is a comfort. "You sound positively terrified."

"I am." It feels good to admit it. *I am, I am, I am.*

"Well," her mother says after a pause, "you're going to try a new doctor. Maybe a woman this time. And then you are going to enroll in school for the fall semester."

"I am?"

"And you'll start coming home, too, every Sunday for dinner. We are still a family. Are you listening to me?"

From a distance, her mother's voice carries on but Tabitha is distracted. She's noticed a lightning bug drifting through her living room on its blinking belly. It dances sadly around the lamp, beating its body repeatedly against the promise of warmth, and light, and home.

How to Speak Czech

Milena wrote in shaking pencil on the backs of used notebook paper everything she planned to make during her granddaughter's visit. Lentil soup, spiced with pepper. Cabbage noodles. Dumplings stuffed with prune butter. Pairs of sweating sausages. A vat of creamed spinach, steaming green and dotted with bread torn ragged from the loaf.

Most of the ingredients she could pick up from the corner market, but her son, Max, made a trip to the grocery store outside of town. He brought back yellow boxes of dry cereal and a gallon of skim milk. A package of Tastykakes. Three frozen dinners, a case of cola, the jumbo can of coffee. "I know my daughter," he said. "This is what my little girl eats."

She was not little anymore, Alema. At thirty-three years old she was still without a husband, though lately she hinted of a beau she refused to bring to Milena's house in Carbon County. Milena placed the cereal and packaged snacks into cabinets and checked the stove. Pancakes with cinnamon for breakfast, a pile of fruit next to the breadbox. Fresh fruit was not something Milena had grown up with in the Czech village. She was raised on slaw, canned milk, dried prunes. Alema would get fruit every day during her visit. She'd eat white bread soft enough to squish between her teeth, noodles buttered until slippery.

"All I'm saying is, don't kill yourself cooking until she gets here and you see how she eats," Max said. "If she even gives herself time to eat."

Milena clasped her hands and paced the length of her kitchen, the shining whiteness of it. The kitchen was all she had left, these days. Life was long, and what did it give her? A husband dead from coal dust, a balding son divorced from his career-driven wife, and a granddaughter with not one, not even two, but three degrees who was driving alone halfway across the country.

And Lida, of course. She still had Lida. Milena walked to the kitchen window and peered through curtains at her sister's duplex next door. Lida would be in there right now, cleaning and straightening, waiting for Alema's arrival so she could swoop in and claim what was never hers.

"I wonder if she'll make it before dark," Max said. "You drive across those prairies at night, and it's like you're about to drop right off the edge of the world." He went over to the cabinet and retrieved the box of Tastykakes.

"I'm about to make lunch," Milena said.

"Just a little snack." Max tore into the box and pulled out a spongy puck, which he put to his mouth again and again until his mustache was plastered with crumbs.

Lida didn't cook. Lida baked. Right now a chocolate layer cake piled high with frosting because that had always been Alema's favorite, as a little girl. Oh, what a girl. Flirty blond hair that flapped around her shoulders and curled even without the puffy pink rollers Lida bought one Christmas. Knees free of scabs, skin so pale she wore long sleeves in the summer and dabs of white on her nose through autumn. Those blue eyes pure like nature: a bunny lost in a field. Bright bathing-suit straps crisscrossing her body, nothing like those heavy woolen suits Lida and Milena wore as youngsters, their hair trapped beneath bathing caps.

Sometimes Lida pretended Alema was hers, that she was a daughter she found curled in a bucket as if by magic instead of being born to Max and that woman he married who couldn't even last as a wife.

Meringue, too. That was another favorite. Lida made the pie light as a dream for Alema, recreating the same pale color of the girl's skin. Mermaid-monster, child of the sea. Alema was raised in Harrisburg, but Lida always knew she would leave that place at the first chance, jump ship. Ship. Chip. Chocolate chips, hot and soft right out of the oven: another memory.

These days, Lida kept the memories stacked and waiting in her oven, as obedient as furled cinnamon rolls. Which Alema only liked without nuts. She was funny that way. Funny also with her friends back then, little girls who spoke a type of language, *slang* Max called it, that Lida didn't understand. Though she and Milena were fast learners of English when they came over. It was good, to be young with another language sitting in your throat: get it out easier.

Alema was a smart one. Came home with *A*s on her report cards and made dioramas filled with tiny people, pets, furniture. She never showed an interest in boys as a child, and even as a teenager, she studied books instead of bringing dates into the parlor or going out to restaurants with white tablecloths, as Lida had done when she was a girl. It was better for Alema to avoid that now. To be smart, and to get the things women of this world were now allowed.

Lida picked up a dishtowel and stared at it, deep in thought. Still. To have a man, a spiced scent floating next to you in the dark, the feeling that he would be the one to catch you in his hands and take you, and claim you, and make you something real.

❧❧❧❧❧

On the first day of her drive from Nebraska to Pennsylvania, Alema allotted herself three stops for food, gas, and restroom breaks. She was accustomed to working a long day straight through. She took an early breakfast at a highway donut shop, brunch in a sub shop, and finally stopped at a truck stop for a longer break, where she sat at the counter with a bottomless cup of coffee while truckers gave her sideways looks. They left her alone, as she knew they would, because she wore tailored dress slacks and a sheer patterned tunic, her hair pulled back in a strawberry bun. She imagined they stepped between their rigs after eating to place bets on her occupation. Psychologist, lawyer, accountant. None would guess she was a microbiologist conducting research at the University of Nebraska, currently comparing plant and animal pathogens. Later, she thought, these men would return to their trucks and remember the line of her neck to make the lonely Midwest miles pass a little sweeter.

She stopped over in Chicago to spend the night with her friend Margi before making the last long leg of the trip. Margi served a late dinner of duck with chardonnay on the ninth-floor balcony and asked about her trip. Alema tried to describe her grandmother's town but came up with nothing but run-down stores, a dying coal industry, and towns spliced with train tracks used only to get to bigger places.

Grandma Milena was a sweet old woman, Alema thought, but she would be better served to leave that creaky duplex and move in with Max in Harrisburg. Lida would have to go too, of course, the sister everyone called crazy but who at least had the sense to never marry. Not that it could have been easy, Alema allowed, considering that Lida and Milena had to suffer through a generation that placed the worth of a woman on husbands and children.

"My grandmother wants to teach me how to cook," Alema told Margi. "She won't take *no* for an answer. So this should be interesting."

Margi looked down at their plates. "It might not be so horrible, to know how to cook," she said. "Maybe you should try."

Alema drank more wine, said nothing. She couldn't explain how heartbreaking it was to watch Milena spend hours bent over that stove, her hands smothered in oven mitts, while everyone else sat there and let her do all the work. Even Alema's own father took advantage of Milena, soaking up the meals without even a *thank you*. That was why Alema had ferried fast food back to the house during her last visit. In that small way, maybe she could bring her grandmother some relief.

"My mother doesn't cook," Alema added. "I must have inherited it from her. She never spent a minute in the kitchen."

"That sounds like your mother," Margi agreed. She stood up and began clearing the plates. She dumped all the dishes in the sink and left them to soak in a sprinkling of dish soap, and then she inflated an air mattress in the corner of the small apartment. Alema watched all of this and remembered that Margi once confided that her mother entered bake-offs and published recipes in their local paper. That world of creation and care seemed so far away, especially there in a high-rise apartment building with an attached deli and grab-and-go café case.

When Margi went to bed, Alema lay in the dark living room thinking of her mother. How she visited Carbon County and was confronted with all that cooking and those Old-World ideas and responded by running away. At least she saved her identity, Alema thought as she drifted off. At least she remained herself.

In the morning, Alema was up at her normal hour of 5 A.M. and had a quick cup of coffee on the balcony. She breathed the city air and took in the buildings, the feeling of morning life. When she left Margi's apartment she obeyed the speed limit and watched the miles tick by one-by-one. The sun came up in front of her as she drove, looping itself over the highway and pulsing in the sky. When it was time to make the trip home the following week, she'd be driving into the sunset. Alema looked forward to that already, the sun fainting in front of her while Pennsylvania spread thin and thinner into nothing.

Milena's kitchen seemed smaller now with this young woman in it. Alema stood tall and thinner than Milena remembered, with a hint of red in her blond hair that had to be the product of chemicals. She was dressed up and polished like a peach pit, even after that long drive. She stood in the kitchen wearing dress slacks, a rich collared shirt, and silver strands of jewelry dangling down her neck.

Milena had on a blue print housedress and her green apron because she was going to make dinner. Hamburgers with onion and a side of cabbage noodles: something easy, unthreatening for her granddaughter's first day. But Alema, it seemed, was already full.

"I ate on the road," Alema said. When Max handed Alema a can of cola and a Tastykake, she accepted each. Opened the wrapping, pulled back the tab. Sugar, chemicals. Milena had firm round onions in the drawer, a package of ground beef waiting in the refrigerator.

"Is that Lida?" Alema asked, and Milena stopped what she was doing to hear the back porch shaking with her sister's footsteps. Lida threw open the kitchen door, rattling the blinds something awful, and made for Alema. She wore her purple cardigan and the gold cross earrings she put on for special occasions, which up until today usually consisted of church and weekly beauty-parlor appointments. She hugged Alema, sending tumbleweeds of perfume through the room.

"I made chocolate cake," Lida said. "Meringue pie. You should see what I made for you." She stood holding Alema's hands, and Alema gripped back.

"I'm here," she said to Lida. "Let's see what you made me."

They went out through the door, Alema brushing lint off the back of the purple cardigan.

✂✂✂✂

To have this girl back in the house again, even if she had turned stern in clothing worn by women lawyers on television. To have this child back again. To have this child. Lida took Alema into her house and through the living room into the kitchen. A small kitchen, not like Milena's. Not built for a family. Built for Lida alone.

Alema admired the cake. Alema smiled at the meringue. Alema so grown up, a plant scientist. A woman scientist, yet no white coat. She wore shoes with a little heel, her pants hemmed perfectly. "You have learned to sew after all," Lida said, but Alema laughed and told her, "I have a tailor."

So. It was true what they said, about women not cooking or cleaning for themselves. It would be nice, to go through life as a man like that. Still. The smell of cake, the whip of meringue. The pride Lida took in how not a whisper of dust could be found within her house, no matter how hard anybody looked.

Alema picked up the pie, its meringue tips dipping like waves. "We should go back to Milena's," she said. "Shouldn't we?"

Lida reached for the cake stand. She was right, that girl. Ever since Max was born, it was Lida going next door to join everyone else in the house with the kitchen table that seated six. Things would not change now. Alema would go back to her father and her grandmother, and Lida would be alone.

On the way out the door, Lida pressed her fingers to the girl's blouse. Silk. Slippery, fine. Alema turned, but how could Lida get the words out. How could she say, *you were the daughter I waited for. You were the life I waited on, and you never belonged to me at all.*

꙳꙳꙳꙳꙳

A few days passed, and still Milena hadn't been able to share any of her cooking secrets with her granddaughter. It was even difficult to get the girl to sit down and eat a decent home-cooked meal. Half the time, Alema wanted chicken in buckets and hoagies wrapped in paper. She picked up pizza dripping in grease from the chain restaurant two towns over that was built to look like a red hat. She ignored the local market and drove herself to the grocery store, bringing back slender cardboard boxes that she stacked in the freezer. Milena read these boxes late at night, hovering outside the freezer while everyone else slept. Lean Cuisine, the stiff cardboard read. She peeled back one of the corners and saw that the contents came in narrow plastic dishes and were nothing but mush.

"We can make lentil soup," Milena said, "with a nice chicken broth and a fresh loaf of bread. Hot and filling. It's easy to make, Alema. You'll see."

Alema was on her cell phone, speaking that complex plant

code and sighing as if the stress of the world was too much for her to bear. "I have to work," she said. "And you shouldn't go through all that trouble. I can just eat some cereal."

Milena turned away and stared at her clean stove. She'd noticed that Alema had eaten one of Lida's scones that morning with her coffee. Milena had watched them, observing Lida's eager hands, and remembered the years she spent raising Max. Lida held him and coddled him, but in the end he always came back to Milena. In the end, Lida returned home to no husband, no children. Always.

⊱⊰⊱⊰⊱⊰

During the day, Alema consulted with colleagues while standing on the front porch where the calls came through most clearly. She had the view of a sad scrub of front lawn, the tumbling chain-link fences, the cracked concrete of a town long gone. At night, she slept in a powder-soft bed in the green guestroom, photographs of her dead grandfather dusting the bureaus. Not a wedding picture of her parents anywhere, she noticed. Grandma Milena had always resented Alema's mother, who spoke three languages and was a journalist-turned-politician. She was still in Harrisburg, busy this week with a campaign, so maybe it was better Alema had come to Carbon County after all.

In the morning, Alema squeaked her way down the staircase and entered the kitchen to find Milena making pancakes. She set a stack in front of Lida and cranked a snowfall of confectioner's sugar across the top.

"Pancakes," Milena said. "Hot breakfast will be good for you. Good for your work."

"I don't know," Alema said doubtfully. "That seems like kind of a heavy breakfast." The pancakes smelled like her childhood, of womanhood. Lida was already at the table cutting a fork through her stack, the utensil buried in softness. She took a bite and smiled.

"You'll have pancakes," Milena said. "At least come watch me make them. What will happen when your husband wants breakfast? I know you think this is impossible, Alema, but it's not. Your father tells me you have a beau. Come sit down and tell us about him."

Alema poured herself a cup of coffee before crossing the kitchen to sit next to Lida. Lida was always alone. Alema wondered if she had a trail of men in her past, maybe even someone like Alema had in Khalid: a man for the nighttime, for the dark. Milena and Lida didn't need to know about Khalid. It was best not to speak of him at all, or mention that he viewed marriage the same way she did. Provincial, sad. Full of dead dreams.

Alema ran her finger across the oilcloth on the table. "He's nobody," she said. "Nobody important." She decided that Lida must sit over there in her duplex and remember past lovers—their hands on her skin, their breath, their smells.

Milena slammed a plate of pancakes down at Alema's place. "Tonight," she said, "I cook. You help."

Alema opened her mouth but her grandmother was already at the kitchen sink, scrubbing dishes. The tie of her apron sat in a bow at the small of her back, her shoulders shaking from her movements. Wash, rinse, dry. In her motions were decades of practice, of cleaning and creating and giving. Alema sat, silenced. Her grandmother clattered dishes in the sink, as strong-willed and stubborn as Khalid or any number of the men Alema had kept company with.

꙾꙾꙾꙾꙾

Milena stood back and surveyed the ingredients she'd piled across her kitchen counters. She had the cabbage chopped and salted, egg noodles ready to boil, prune butter and bread and spinach lined up in a row. She had the clean wooden cutting board, the knives, the gingham dishtowels, and the spoons. Bowls. Plates. Pots and pans and butter.

Max sat at the table like a spectator who had bought a ticket. He told Alema, "My money's on Grandma," and laughed. Lida was there, too, this time with no dessert. She sat next to Max with her hands folded, as if waiting for the church organ to pound its song into the air.

Alema, who stood cross-armed in the corner, had put on a skirt and heels. She did that on purpose, Milena thought. She was just the same as a child: wild and fierce headed, strong. "I don't cook," Alema was saying. "I order out. I go to restaurants." She paused, sly. "People cook for me."

"Like your boyfriend, I bet," Max said. "Maybe you're on to something. Have the man cook." He stayed at the table, waiting to be served. Her lovely, lovely son. Milena watched as Lida reached over to pat his arm. She wanted to fly across the table to hold Lida back, to remind her that this was not hers, that she was barren and single. But she did not. She went to the counter instead, picked up a knife and began cutting carrots.

"Alema, come," she said. "Start putting spinach in the pot. You can brown flour, no?"

Alema walked to the stove, picked up a wooden spoon. A pile of flour sat in a frying pan, waiting. She looked at it.

"Turn it on," Milena said, pressing her granddaughter to light a burner under the flour. "Now keep moving it with the spoon. Like this. See?"

Alema moved the pan to stare at the flame as if she did not trust fire in the house. Milena dabbed prune butter onto dough and dropped cabbage into noodles. Condensed milk for the spinach, celery for the lentils.

Alema fumbled with the pepper and sneezed into her arm. She wiped her hands on the back of her skirt and held them up, empty. Milena sighed and moved around her granddaughter as if she were no longer there. Lentil soup simmering, dumplings bubbling with prune filling. Spinach hugging the pot with green eagerness, the egg noodles quivering with butter and that homely cabbage scent. Hours of it, this cooking. Through it all, Alema stumbled around the stove, dodging dumplings and crying out when steam struck her skin. Her own granddaughter could not follow a recipe, Milena realized, and certainly could not cook from memory. These meals came to Milena through her very body, just as they did to her mother, and her mother before that. Alema was more like a bird, hollow boned and flighty, startled by butter and salt.

When it was over and Max and Lida had full plates before them at the table, Alema busied herself at the sink, fighting a stain on her blouse. Milena rounded up a spoon. "You try," she said, and dipped into the lentil soup. She held out the spoon for her granddaughter. At first, Alema stood apart from Milena, but then she leaned forward and accepted a bite.

"It's good," Alema said, as if surprised. She looked at the spoon, clean now from her own hunger.

"It always was," Milena told her.

୬୧୬୧୬୧

That one bite started everything. The food was soft on Alema's tongue, substantial and sticky with home—her grandmother's home, not her mother's untouched stainless-steel kitchen with the dishwasher camouflaged as a cabinet. Alema took a second, tentative bite and felt something inside her bloom.

"Go on," Milena urged. "Eat."

So she did. Alema took the spoon from Milena and moved from dish to dish, eating directly from the pots and pans. It was like the food was undressing her. The lentils peeled off her shirt, the sausages tugged her skirt down to her knees. Prune butter removed her shoes and stockings and spinach pulled her hair down from its bun. She couldn't stop. She gathered speed and began eating so fast that spittle and bits of food collected at her mouth.

"Honey," Max said, standing up. "Slow down. You'd think we've been starving you this whole time."

Alema shook her head. This food was a comfort, a memory, a weapon. She finished her spoonful of spinach and turned to the prune dumplings. She grabbed a fork and pierced three in succession. They tasted buttery, warm.

"Alema," Max said. He was standing at her shoulder, and she wondered how he'd gotten there so quickly. Her father was weighty and unwieldy, not a sneak. She looked at his thinning hair, the shiny patches on his skin. And the mustache—no one had mustaches anymore. He put his hand on her shoulder and she felt the heat of him, the pulse beneath his palm.

"Let her eat," Milena said. She stood at the table, next to Lida's chair, with her arms crossed. Alema wiped her eyes. She still felt naked, pulled apart by the food, but Milena stood at attention, prepared to start cooking again if Alema ate every morsel. And if Alema ate the second batch, Milena would simply make more.

It was an unending stream of nourishment, and Alema had allowed herself to go hungry for too long.

⋇⋇⋇⋇⋇

Milena turned off the stove. She was sore, wiped out from all the cooking and had cleaning ahead of her yet. She covered the pot of still-simmering spinach and rolled the dumplings into a covered container. Alema had finally eaten her fill. At least Milena had done that much for her.

Milena sighed, not unhappily, at her messy kitchen. "*To byl ale den*," she said, and then stood back in surprise. She and Lida never spoke Czech anymore. There was no place for it in this world. But once the words came out of Milena's mouth, she was glad.

Alema looked up from her place at the table, where she sat in a daze after her binge. "What did you say?" she asked.

"I said it's about time you stopped acting like a little child." Milena spoke in Czech, and she savored every word. Alema leaned toward the language as if it could save her.

Lida shook her head. "This is your only granddaughter," she

said. "*Ty jsi ale nevděčná*. You should be happy she came all the way to see you."

"*Nic ti do toho není*," Milena replied. The Czech flowed from her effortlessly, as if she'd never stopped speaking it. She smiled in spite of herself. Here, at last, was their language, and it sounded natural even after all those years.

"So ungrateful," Lida added. "You don't deserve such a granddaughter."

"You don't know what it means to have a grandchild," Milena said. "All your life, you've tried to take over my family. You put yourself right in with everyone else, as if you belong. But you don't."

Alema was watching them closely. "Tell me what you're saying."

"*Teď ne*," Milena told her. "Not now."

"You never let me have anything," Lida said. Her voice was quiet. She looked down at the table and didn't direct her words to anyone in particular, but she spoke in Czech, so she meant them for Milena. "I had nothing, my whole life, and still you are prepared to take more away from me. And now," Lida continued, "what you have is a granddaughter whose biggest fear is becoming you."

Alema closed her eyes. "It's a strange language. Kind of coarse, but beautiful. I wish I understood it." She looked up at Milena. "Teach me to say something."

"Not now," Milena said again. She turned back to the sink and picked up a sponge.

"I'll teach you," Lida told Alema. "What do you want to say?"

Alema murmured something indecipherable. Milena glanced back to see Alema and Lida close together, their heads almost touching across the table.

Finally, Alema pulled away. "*Babičko*," she said. Milena froze. Alema rarely called her "Grandmother" even in English. Usually she called her nothing at all.

"*Děkuji*," Alema went on haltingly. She glanced at Lida, who nodded her on in encouragement. She tried again: "*Děkuji*."

Milena looked down at her hands. She wanted to say *Děkuji* in return, to send the thanks right back to Alema, but she couldn't. So she said nothing.

"Here," Alema said. She looked pleased with herself for the few Czech words she'd managed. "Let me do something for you." She pushed back her chair and walked over to the breadbox, where she produced a pile of spice muffins.

"Lida made these this morning," Alema said, passing the muffins around the table. When Milena hesitated, Alema waved one in front of her. "How do you say, *This is for you?*"

Milena took the muffin even though she'd baked a white cake that was sitting on the adjacent counter. No one noticed it, but maybe that didn't matter.

"*To je pro tebe*," Milena said. She looked at Lida, who sat beside Alema but alone nonetheless. "This is for you."

"Say it again," Alema said. "Slower."

"*To je pro tebe*." Milena met Lida's eyes as she brought the soft spice muffin to her lips. This is for you. She sank into it deep, its powdery texture filling her throat, creating inside her space for all that was generous, and giving, and good.

The Wig Shop

On Saturday morning, Margot's mother lies down for twenty minutes to *recharge,* which means humming Sinatra songs at the ceiling until she feels well enough to stand. Margot waits in her bedroom, by the window, and cleans the bristles of her hairbrush. She pulls the strands out one by one and lets them drift outside onto the breeze. When her mother is finally ready to go, Margot follows her downstairs, determined for at least the course of this shopping trip to forget about the hairbrush, and the loose strands floating outside, and hair in general. Then she remembers that this will be impossible.

"Maybe afterward, we'll get frozen yogurt," her mother says once they're in the car. She puts the key in the ignition and shakes the minivan to life. "Doesn't that sound good?"

Margot nods and off they go. She thinks of the frozen-yogurt shop, how it's always so cold in there, and how she and her mother both favor the little table by the window. Only once did they skip the table and get their yogurt to go—when Margot was ten, and her mother gave her the talk about periods. They took their yogurt cups back to the car, and Margot clutched hers, no longer hungry, as her mother explained cramp remedies and monthly cycles. As far as Margot was concerned, they might as well have been discussing the moon. On second thought, maybe they were.

Today, her mother fiddles with the radio as they drive, and Margot looks down at her hands. She does not want to know how to get to a wig shop and is in fact surprised that their town has such a store at all. If things had worked out with UCLA, she would be packing for California right now. Instead, she is stuck in the only state she's known, a keystone full of forests and farmland and a handful of cities that are always too far away.

Margot looks out the window and sees water. They are on a bridge crossing the Susquehanna River, and she squints at the riverbanks. Going over this bridge once felt like flying. Now she sees it will only take them into town, to a shop that will sell her mother synthetic hair and maybe, if they are lucky, a little bit of hope.

"You'd think," her mother says, "there'd be a better system in place than this."

"What do you mean?" Margot thinks her mother is talking about the bridge, the river. She looks down again and sees the water stretch on into the distance, silent and still.

"Chemotherapy. Wigs. It all seems so ridiculous."

"Oh." Margot leans back in her seat. Stupid of her, to think her mother meant the river. Stupid of her to think anything could remain as simple as a current that travels in one direction. When she was a girl she was in awe of that river, convinced of its power and strength, but she knows better now.

The Susquehanna is nothing but a thin blue line wrapping its way toward other thin blue lines, useless and weak and filled with exasperating hope.

❧❧❧❧❧

The wig shop is a tiny operation on King Street, in a part of town Margot only knows for its coffee shops and the lone art gallery. Inside, the store is dimly lit, and the wigs sit on Styrofoam heads on shelves lining the walls. Right away, Margot sees that they are arranged for two different types of customers: the sensible wigs in muted blonds and browns, and then the section of hot pinks and purples with spikes of glitter combed through. Those are the fun wigs. Those are the wigs for people who are not dying.

Margot and her mother are the only people in the store except for the clerk, a pear-shaped woman named Francine who wears a long, flowing skirt and a nametag decorated with a smiley-face sticker.

"Hello," Francine says. "First time here?"

Margot's mother nods. She walks in a careful arc toward the wigs, as if assessing whether they will attack. Slowly, she reaches out and touches the golden locks of a wig so long it almost brushes against the floor.

Francine studies them for a moment. "It's cancer," she guesses. "You have cancer."

Nothing could be more obvious, Margot thinks. Her mother wears a scarf to hide the way her hair has fallen out, and her eyebrows are drawn on with an eyeliner pencil. Surely Francine sells wigs to cancer patients all the time, which makes her question even worse. Margot wants to walk over to Francine, knock the wig comb out of her hands, and set her straight.

What Margot wants to say to Francine is this: *Yes, my mother has cancer. But she's not like those other people who come in here for wigs. My mother will survive.*

❧❧❧❧❧

Margot's mother tries on a dozen wigs and Margot can tell she hates them all, even the one she eventually decides to buy. It's a short blond shag, sensible and not too far from what her real hair once looked like.

"Maybe you should get one, too," her mother says, staring at herself in the mirror before looking up to catch Margot's eyes. "You could pretend to be a whole new person when you go off to college."

In less than two months, Margot will move into a dorm room at Bridgeville University, a state school an hour's drive away on back roads that twist between cornfields. By the time college notifications started making the rounds, her mother's cancer had already struck. Margot picked Bridgeville as if blindfolded with her arms reaching straight out into the dark. While her friends went shopping for dorm supplies and built up a nervous energy about moving to new cities and states, Margot stayed up late browsing medical information online. She memo-rized facts about malignant tumors, T-cell counts, survival rates. She read about oncologists who had gotten cancer themselves. If they died, she counted the number of children they had; if they lived, she counted the years they'd been cancer-free. It was always under ten.

With her fingertips only, Margot touches a red-brown wig with curls made from real hair. For the first time, she pictures the disease in her own body. She has her mother's currents, her mother's cancer curled and sleeping in her midsection. Maybe it started that long-ago day with the frozen yogurt, when they first admitted to each other that they had bodies, uteruses, ovaries. Now it waits inside her, like the river frozen over in the winter. One day it would thaw, cracking apart piece by piece.

"Will that be all?" Francine sweeps her hand through the air to indicate so much more is available. Margot's mother sets the wig on the counter and opens her purse.

"That's it," she says.

Margot knows her mother doesn't plan to be sick enough to need another wig. This is a one-shot deal. Once this transaction is complete, they will be free to step back into a world of sunlight and people alive with plans. They are one signature, one receipt slip away from this place. Already it feels like a bad memory.

But when Margot's mother holds out her credit card, Francine grabs her firmly by the wrist.

"You will get through this," Francine says, and her voice is soft, but there is a fierceness there, too. "You'll make it. You have to."

Francine pulls her closer, until Margot's mother is leaning halfway across the counter. Margot knows she should do something, but she feels paralyzed by Francine's words, wants to hold still until she's spoken every last one.

"I tell this to all my customers," Francine goes on. "These goddamn doctors. You can't trust any of them. So do yourself a favor and don't. You can recover, and you will. It's your choice."

Francine lets go and zips the credit card through the slot on the cash register. Margot's mother leaves her arm hanging in the air where Francine had grabbed it. She looks like she's trying to hold onto those words, or at least believe them.

By the time she's rung up the wig and packed it neatly into a box, Francine is all smiles again. "You let me know if you need anything else," she says, and then turns to Margot. She narrows her eyes to size her up, as if reading her future. "That goes for you too, honey."

"Thanks," Margot says, or thinks she says. She can't remember if the word actually came out of her mouth. She's thinking instead of Francine's expression when she grabbed her mother's hand, the way she acted like all this could be wished away if only they wanted it enough.

As they leave, Margot looks back to see Francine combing one of the wigs. She does this lovingly, gently, as if her hands can bring life to whatever she holds.

✼✼✼✼✼

Once outside, they blink at the sun and hover dumbly outside the wig shop, as if they left something valuable behind but are afraid to go back in.

"She's right, you know," Margot's mother says. "I'll be fine. I won't need this for long." She shakes the bag that holds her new hair.

Of course she will. This is the woman who snapped back after her hysterectomy to jog three miles a day, who threw the neighborhood's biggest graduation party, and who insisted on visiting every college alongside Margot, even when she got shaky or short of breath.

This is the mother who once bought her daughter a chocolate frozen yogurt and sat with her in the car to talk about puberty. They didn't even drive anywhere; Margot remembers that now. They sat in the parking lot and Margot stared at the car in front of her while her mother went over things she mostly knew. Because that's how it goes: by the time parents get around to telling you the important things, you've already figured them out.

"I lied about UCLA," Margot says.

"What?" Her mother looks up, and the sun shines so brightly on the scarf wrapped against her scalp that Margot worries the cloth will become transparent and reveal its secret.

"I got in, but I didn't tell you. It's all right," Margot continues, but inside she feels the loss all over again. "California is too far anyway."

Her mother turns away to take a labored breath. "It's not all right, Margot. You're ruining your future because of me."

"Nothing's ruined. I'm still going to college."

"A lousy school in this lousy state. Isn't that how you first described it when I suggested you apply there?"

Margot doesn't say anything.

"It isn't my choice, for you to see this," her mother goes on. "For you to take care of me."

"I know."

"UCLA was your dream, Margot."

"I know."

"And you're giving it up for me, because I'm—" but she stops. She closes her mouth and sets it in a line. Margot watches her mother's face, that blank expression created by the absence of eyelashes and eyebrows. She won't say it. She will never say it, not even right at the end, when Margot is leaning over a hospital bed somewhere, counting down the last breaths.

The sun is hot on the sidewalk. Margot shields her eyes against the brightness. "You still want that frozen yogurt?"

Her mother shakes her head. "I changed my mind," she says. "I want to go home."

They get back in the car and cross the bridge again. Margot doesn't tell her mother that she deferred the acceptance and can transfer next fall. She doesn't mention this because what might set her free to California is the same thing she has feared since the day Dr. Rhinehart gave them the diagnosis. It's better if she doesn't say these words out loud. It's better if she sits still and watches the water pass beneath them in its inevitable current.

Somewhere down that river is the future, the sad dream of California come true. But for now Margot sits in the passenger seat, a wig on the floor by her feet, and she lets her mother drive her the whole way home.

Return to Stillbrook Farm

It was all the same, right down to the maroon paint on the stable's Dutch doors, but it was the smell inside that took Caroline back: dirt and hay and manure, the musk of a horse freshly dappled with rain. She walked deeper into the barn with Denise trailing behind her. Caroline had changed into jeans and boots, but Denise was still in the outfit she'd worn to the airport: tapered wool pants, a blazer, and flat brown loafers that were completely inappropriate for a barn. Denise was a smoker; Caroline had learned that of her mother's partner within the first ten minutes of their meeting, and now Caroline worried something in the woman's clothes would spark and set the whole place up. The corner of dry hay, the wooden stalls, the horse hair just waiting to singe.

A stable was a place full of risk and heartbreak and the potential for disaster. If she had learned nothing else growing up, she had learned this.

Caroline glanced into the trophy room on her way down the barn aisle. She saw a wall full of dusty ribbons, the championship ones so long they almost brushed the floor. Some of the ribbons might even be her own, won ages ago. Framed newspaper articles and a trophy shelf lined the far wall. If she stopped to look, she'd see photographs of her mother smiling from under a velvet hunt cap, holding up her latest prize. Instead, Caroline passed the trophy room and kept walking until she reached the right stall. She knew it by the brass plaque nailed to the door: *Venus,* it read. *Joyce Anderson, owner.*

Caroline ran her fingers along her mother's name. When she was growing up, she'd count the number of her mother's plaques on the stalls, proof that Joyce Anderson loved horses and made her life working with them. In the week since Joyce's death, however, the ownership line on Venus's plaque had become outdated. Everyone knew this: from Denise, who had found Joyce lying in the ditch by the far pasture, to Venus, the mare who had put her there in the first place.

"Your mother loved that horse," Denise said from behind her. "She loved her more than anything."

She loved her more than me, Caroline thought.

Caroline peered in the stall and gave the bay Hanoverian mare an appraising look. Venus nodded her head a few times, perhaps hoping for a treat. It had been eleven years since Caroline moved away. Back then, Venus was still a filly full of nips and kicks. She spooked easily and didn't take to a halter right away, so Caroline's mother spent hours out in the round pen working with her. Even then it was clear: Venus was a priority.

Caroline held out her hand, palm up with the fingers held together. The mare approached and sniffed, blowing in and out, her breath a hot assault. Venus's coat was shiny and sleek, her mane straightened of snarls, her hooves evenly trimmed and polished. This horse was a superstar in the show ring and could bring in upward of tens of thousands of dollars if sold.

"I'd like to see where my mother fell," Caroline said.

Denise fiddled with a button on her blazer and looked down the empty stable aisle. "All right," she said at last. She seemed disoriented, probably still in shock from Joyce's death. "But it's a bit of a walk."

Denise led the way out of the barn and to the main pasture, which stretched alongside the stable and rose up a hill, disappearing into a drop on the other side. A gray barn cat snaked through the heat and high grass nearby. In the years Caroline had lived in Philadelphia, the only cat she'd known was Bingo, her former roommate's black-and-white house cat. Bingo was fat, lethargic, and domesticated out of his mind. Barn cats, meanwhile, were a breed of their own. In Caroline's childhood, they'd always been present: scrawny, tough creatures who appeared at unpredictable times with battle scars and wounds, the price of their independence. Joyce doted on them in private; more than once, Caroline caught her mother hidden in a dark corner of the stable, holding out pieces of chicken or fish. The cats lapped the treats out of her hand, momentarily forgetting their wildness.

"This way," Denise said, and they turned to head uphill. Caroline let Denise lead her as if giving a tour, as if this whole place wasn't ingrained in Caroline's memory. It was more Denise's home now, anyway. Joyce had described the changes she and Denise made to the stable over the years: the new wash rack, a change in the pasture layout. She had to explain these things over the phone or through letters, because Caroline worked for years to round up enough excuses to not visit the farm.

Now there would be no more updates from her mother, no more requested visits or promises Caroline inevitably would break. This fact made Caroline pause and blink into the sun. She glanced away to see a red roan standing in the adjacent pasture, its mottled belly stretched tight and full.

Denise came back a few steps. "Pregnant," she said of the mare. "Your mother was excited about that one."

Caroline nodded, calmed by the sight of the big bland animal facing them, a few strands of grass poking out of the corner of the horse's mouth.

"It's not much farther," Denise said. She touched the back of Caroline's wrist, briefly, and then moved away. They reached the top of the hill, where Caroline paused to survey the rolling pastureland. The trees, green and full of summer, swayed their shadows across the ground. She remembered how Joyce sometimes left the arena to ride through a field or pasture, for the change of scenery. It was something they had shared. When, as a child, Caroline grew frustrated with a jump course or dressage test, Joyce would send her out for a hack around the farm. She wondered what Joyce had been struggling with when she decided to ride Venus out here.

"It's just down there," Denise said, pointing to the bottom of the hill. "Venus must have taken off and your mother fell at the bottom."

"My mother didn't fall off," Caroline said. "Venus must have thrown her."

Denise didn't have a reply for that. Caroline looked at the shallow ditch at the bottom of the grassy hill. That was where her mother had landed, where she had twisted her neck. Caroline started down the hill. She could hear Denise stumbling behind her, picking her way down without a hint of grace, as Caroline tracked through the deep grass without effort. She had been the one to run off to Philadelphia while Denise lived here with her mother for eleven years, but that didn't change their roles. Denise was the uncertain city girl while Caroline moved through a pasture as if she was born for it, with or without a horse beneath her.

When she reached the bottom, Caroline slowed to a walk and circled the area surrounding the ditch, the place her mother lay dying. Denise finally caught up, breathing hard. Caroline scanned the ditch and the fence line before directing her gaze toward the top of the hill, where she could make out the silhouette of the pregnant roan flicking her tail to reach the flies. That horse stood on her feet all day, bearing a tremendous weight, all with the purpose to keep what was inside her belly kicking and alive.

"Maybe you'd like to be alone," Denise said. She opened one side of her blazer and fanned herself. "I'm not really dressed to be out here."

"All right," Caroline said. "I'll come in soon."

Denise headed back up the pasture, slipping on the grass in her flat shoes. The hill was strong and coated in long salty grass. It was the type of hill Caroline and her mother had ridden up and down on horseback for years. No way did Joyce Anderson, show rider and horse breeder, fall off for no reason. Venus had thrown her.

Once Denise was gone, Caroline sat down in the ditch and folded her legs to the side. The day was wearing on, but it was still hot. She could hear the continuous drum of insects and, if she listened carefully, the sound of horses ripping grass from the ground.

She ran her hand lightly over the grass in the spot her mother had fallen. Joyce's last living moments had happened here, with that open blue sky staring down at her. Caroline pictured Denise stumbling down the pasture to find Joyce lying crooked on the ground. Then she thought about Venus, standing mere feet away with the reins askew across her neck, patiently waiting for Joyce to die.

⋇⋇⋇⋇⋇

Denise and Joyce had met during Caroline's senior year of high school. Of course, neither Caroline nor her father knew anything about it in the beginning. Caroline was more concerned with college acceptances than her mother's personal life.

When the admissions letter from Temple University came two weeks after Caroline's eighteenth birthday, she clutched the letter to her chest and ran to the west paddock, where she assumed she could find her mother working with Venus. She was right.

"Good, you can help," Joyce said when Caroline appeared.

Caroline climbed the fence rails and dropped down on the other side.

"Careful," Joyce warned. "Don't spook her."

"Everything spooks Venus," Caroline said. The filly responded by flipping her head back, letting her downy new mane shake at the sky. Caroline held up her letter. "I need to talk to you."

Joyce handed Caroline the lead. "Walk her around for a minute, will you? I need to see how she moves. I've been too close to her."

Caroline took the lead. "Mom. I got into Temple."

"But that's in Philadelphia." Joyce clapped her hands, sending Venus into a skittish walk.

"What's your point?"

"There are plenty of schools in Virginia with better equestrian programs. Wait until you hear from Hollins, at least."

Caroline tugged at Venus' halter. "Temple was my first choice."

"Don't pull. Take her for a quick trot so I can see her stride."

Caroline grasped the lead and broke into a jog, dragging a reluctant Venus along with her. "I can't keep doing this," she said.

"You're doing fine." Joyce shaded her eyes and smiled as Venus trotted by. "Look at that conformation. She's going to be fabulous, I can just tell."

"No, *this*," Caroline said, and came to a stop. Venus, surprised by the abrupt change, tossed her head again. "I can't keep living in the middle of nowhere."

Joyce lowered her hand. "Give me that letter," she said. "And keep Venus moving. You're confusing her."

Caroline walked Venus to her mother and slapped the acceptance letter into her hands. "They gave me a scholarship."

Her mother glanced at the letter. "I said, keep her moving."

Caroline jerked into a run, pulling Venus behind her.

Joyce folded the letter again. "You're not going to Philadelphia. You wouldn't be happy there."

"You mean you wouldn't be happy if I left."

"Give me the lead. I'll take her from here."

Caroline walked over to her mother and snatched the acceptance letter away before handing over the lead rope, as if they were an even trade. Her mother reached up to stroke Venus' neck.

"You think you're the only one who wants to leave?" Joyce said. She clucked to Venus and began leading her in a broad circle throughout the paddock. She didn't say anything else to Caroline when she led Venus past. Her expression turned guilty, as if she'd let something slip by accident.

Caroline fell silent. Her mother loved the stable and the life she had built from it. She certainly loved Venus, more than any of the other horses combined. So what she had said didn't make sense. It made so little sense, in fact, that Caroline didn't see the point in thinking about it any longer.

"I'm leaving," Caroline said. She slipped through the fence rails and walked toward the barn, where her horse Sport was recuperating in his stall. He'd come in from the pasture a few days ago with long gashes in his legs, the work of tiny hooves.

Caroline stepped into Sport's stall and cradled his big head. The vet wasn't sure when he could compete again. Caroline had built her entire life of showing in preparation for this summer, the last summer she'd be home. She and Sport had done well last year, but intense training through the fall and winter had made them better than ever. Even Joyce had once doubted that Sport had it in him to be a top eventer—he was a jumper, but not a natural talent at dressage—but through hard work and love, Caroline had proven her wrong.

Sport sighed and rested his head against Caroline's chest. She stroked the broad flat space between his eyes. It had been Joyce's idea to turn him out with Venus. She did this because Sport was gentle with foals, tolerant of their mischief. Joyce trusted Sport. That was all that mattered to her—that Sport wouldn't hurt Venus, and that her baby would be safe, free to grow strong and become a winner. It didn't matter if that left Caroline in a dark stable on a warm spring day, dressing leg wounds when she should have been training.

Caroline wrapped her arms around Sport's neck and hugged. "I'm going to miss you," she said. And she already did. She knew, with Sport's warm hairs against her cheek, that once she finally left for college, things would change.

What she didn't know was that it would take her eleven years to return, and only then, for her mother's funeral.

❧❧❧❧

The memorial service was held in the small country church located about ten miles from the farm. This meant that Joyce's family and friends had to travel for miles along desolate farm roads, passing pastures full of thick-necked cows and roadside stands weighed down with bright produce. There was nowhere better to have the service or reception, Denise and Caroline told each other as they waited for the guests to find the church. Joyce's parents were both dead, her sisters were scattered in different cities, and her ex-husband Tom certainly wasn't going to play host.

He showed up for the service, though. Caroline knew it was her father from the hurried way he pulled into the parking lot, the quick slam of his door. She told Denise to wait in the church, and then she stepped outside. It was another sunny day, and she held her hand to her forehead as she watched her father walk up the church steps.

"Sweetheart," he said, and took her in a hug. "How awful this must be for you."

He meant more than Joyce's death, Caroline knew. After they heard the news, Tom took the train from New York to Philadelphia to spend a few days with Caroline to comfort her. The awful thing he was referring to now, Caroline assumed, was Denise.

"They still have rooms at the Holiday Inn," he said. "We could call right now and reserve one for you. I'll pay."

Caroline looked down and followed the line of her skirt hem. She was wearing a dark gray dress, only a few shades from black. Her mother had looked beautiful in dark gray. In fact, Joyce had worn a gray turtleneck one of the last times Caroline had seen her.

"I'm staying with Denise," she said. "The house has four bedrooms. Remember?"

Her father looked away at the mention of Denise's name. "All right," he said. "Whatever you want."

They entered the church. Denise's entire family had shown up, a crowd of mousey-looking, serious people who huddled in the corner. Caroline took it upon herself to walk over and shake each person's hand while Denise stood back and checked her cell phone. Tom, meanwhile, settled himself in the front pew as if he and Joyce had never divorced.

Caroline didn't recognize the pastor who delivered the eulogy, but he seemed to know Joyce well. He told a story about being invited over for dinner—he was careful not to mention Denise,

Caroline noticed—and finding Joyce standing in the middle of a smoky kitchen, waving oven mitts to get the smoke detector to stop ringing. Then he mentioned some charity work she did for the county animal shelter, and finally he turned to the subject of horses. Caroline tried to tune this part out but nonetheless heard him point out that riding was Joyce's one true joy and that no one would forget how much she loved her favorite horse, Venus.

After the eulogy, each of Joyce's sisters stood up to say a few words. Caroline remained seated. Her aunts had asked her to prepare something to say, but she had declined. She closed her eyes instead and pictured Venus, riderless and running.

At the reception, they crowded into the drab church basement that featured a black-and-yellow-checkered floor and curtains hung on windowless walls. Guests served themselves from a buffet. Canned beets, pickles, hard rolls, slices of roast beef, pasta salad, and puff pastries—it was a strange combination, but Caroline took some of everything. When her paper plate sagged with food, she found her father seated at a long folding table. She pulled up a metal chair and joined him.

Tom didn't have any food in front of him. Caroline gave him a deviled egg from her plate. He spent a long moment holding it in his hand, the way no one holds a deviled egg. It rested completely in his palm, cupped as if he didn't care whether the slimy yellow filling would rub off on his skin.

"I was just thinking," he said, "that this is twice now."

"What do you mean?"

"Twice that Venus took her away." He looked at the egg.

Caroline sat quietly for a moment. "Don't you think Denise had something to do with the first time?"

Tom turned to look at the corner where Denise sat, protected by a table full of her relatives. Caroline could see the lines on her face, the sadness marked into her skin.

"True," he said. "But Denise sure didn't have anything to do with this. That animal was always unpredictable. I knew it from the start."

Caroline used her fork to move some beets around her plate. They left red trails and stained the rest of her food. She hadn't seen Venus since that first day, when Denise took her to the pasture. For the most part, she and Denise had stayed in the house, where they cooked enough food for the week and talked about sorting through Joyce's things without actually getting around to it. Every time Denise went to the barn—often to check on the roan, who was about ready to give birth—Caroline made an excuse to stay inside. She read or watched movies on the couch, wrapping herself in a rust-colored afghan she learned Denise had made for Joyce last Christmas.

"What we should do," he said, "is have that horse put down. Just end it now. Christ, all she's caused us." He maneuvered the deviled egg to his mouth and took a messy bite.

"That's ridiculous," Caroline told him, but she had thought of the same thing.

"Let's hope Denise at least has the sense to sell her," he said. "Though it seems unfair that she would be the one to get all the money, if I understand the circumstances of the will. You deserve something. You're the one who shared horses with your mother. Not Denise."

"That's true," Caroline said. "But I don't need anything. You know that." In fact, she was relieved that Denise would come into possession of the house and property. Joyce had left Caroline some money, her wedding china, and the contents of the stable's trophy room, among a few other things of little consequence. Caroline just wanted to return to Philadelphia and let her childhood home dissolve behind her, like a mirage.

Tom started to answer, but his words were overpowered by music. One of the sisters had brought a portable stereo and began playing some of Joyce's favorite songs. First "Hey Jude," then "Heart of Gold," and finally "Sweet Caroline," the song that had inspired Joyce in naming Caroline. Only a few years ago, Neil Diamond admitted he wrote that song after seeing a photograph of a young Caroline Kennedy riding her pony on the White House lawn.

As the songs played on, Denise came bustling over, her cell phone pressed in her hand.

"The roan," Denise said. She rarely called the horses by their names, instead referring to them as if they were nothing but colors: the roan, the gray, the brown-and-white spotted lesson pony. "That was Sherry. The roan's getting ready to give birth. We have to go."

"Now?" Caroline looked around. Most of the other guests were leaving. Her father was gathering his coat, pointedly not looking in their direction.

"We have to," Denise said. "Sherry says it doesn't look good."

"Fine." Caroline threw her soggy plate in the trash and searched for the pastor to thank him. She'd have to say goodbye to her father and wish him a safe trip home. There were flowers, too, dozens of bouquets she and Denise planned to load into the back of the pickup truck. Something to brighten the house, Denise had said. But Caroline didn't see how that was possible. It was so dark, inside and out, and everything in Denise's house felt shadowed and lost: thrown to the ground without another thought.

❧❧❧❧

While they waited for the emergency on-call vet to arrive, Denise and Caroline sat in the straw at the struggling roan's head. The mare lay on her side and made groaning sounds. There was no sign of the foal appearing from the birth canal. Now they had nothing to do but wait.

"Damn vet," Denise said. "She could die by the time he gets here."

Caroline stroked the mare's neck as a dreary childhood memory came back to her. Her first horse had been a chestnut Welsh pony named Cimarron. Cimarron had a wide blaze running down his face, a fondness for peppermints, and the worst luck with colic. One night, when Cimarron had a particularly bad case, the vet was caught up in other emergencies and wasn't able to come for hours. Caroline and her mother spent all night walking Cimarron up and down the barn aisle to keep him from rolling in his stall, which could be fatal for a colicky horse. Caroline still remembered the sweat on his neck and the way he twisted to nip at his stomach while they took turns walking him up and down, up and down. The vet finally did come, and Cimarron was back to himself by the next day.

It wasn't until a year later, when Cimarron came down with colic in the middle of the night and no one was there to notice, that he died.

Caroline put her head in her hands. It was too much to

handle, the way everything could go wrong without warning. The way people and horses could fail you at any moment and go and do something stupid like dying all alone, in secret.

The roan let out another pained sound. A horse in a nearby stall responded with a low whinny. It was Venus. Caroline couldn't see anything except the roan's head and her high, round stomach, but she knew it was Venus calling out. It spooked her, to think of the mare hovering in the barn's shadows, again a witness to suffering.

Denise pulled out a pack of cigarettes and rolled it between her hands.

"You can't smoke in here," Caroline said.

Denise glanced at her sideways. "I know that," she said. "You think your mother would let me smoke anywhere near the barn? Once I lit up about ten feet from the entrance and she let me have it." Denise cracked open the pack and peered inside, then closed it again. "This is my last pack," she said. "And not three cigarettes left in it. If that makes a difference to you."

The gravel outside the barn crackled with the weight of a truck. Denise put her cigarettes away and sat back against the wall with a sigh, as if the hard part were already over.

"What do we have here?" The vet entered the stall and went right to the mare. Denise introduced him to Caroline as Dr. Wysoki. He was a short man, round in the middle and balding up top, and he laid soft, white hands against the roan.

The foal was presenting breech, which Dr. Wysoki explained was not necessarily serious. Even so, he looked concerned, and when the foal's back hooves started to appear—wrapped in an eerie, whitish sack—he struggled to arrange the foal in the best position. He even reached inside the roan with his hand.

"Here we go," he said as the rest came sliding out. He worked to tear open the sack that surrounded the squirming foal. "Hold that mare down, now. We can't have her stand up too soon."

But it was too late. The roan, disoriented from the birth, tossed her head and started to her feet. Caroline reached to push the mare back but the umbilical cord ruptured, sending blood gushing to the ground.

"Damn it." Dr. Wysoki clamped the ends of the cord and started working on the mare. Caroline looked away. As a child, she was largely uninvolved in the breeding process and viewed the whole thing as messy and mysterious. Now, she turned her head from the mare and tried to remember her as she'd been only days ago, standing hot and heavy in the pasture.

Dr. Wysoki finally sat back, sweating. The foal lay slick and heavy headed on the ground. The roan had calmed down. She moved toward her foal and sniffed cautiously.

"A colt," he said. He wiped his face. "Seems to be in pretty good shape, considering."

"What about her?" Caroline asked, stroking the roan's face.

Dr. Wysoki looked at the mare. "She'll live," he said.

Denise let out a breath. "Your mother would have been so happy," she told Caroline. She smiled at the foal, who was already attempting to struggle to his feet. "She had been looking forward to this for a long time."

Caroline looked down at the bloodied straw. Venus called out again from her own stall. This time, she sounded lonely. As if she had been calling out this way every night for the last week and was still awaiting a response.

❧❧❧❧❧

Caroline's phone beeped as she and Denise were still watching over the roan and her foal. She pulled her phone from her pocket to find a text message from her father. *I'm here,* it read. *Is the horse okay?*

Caroline stood up, brushing straw from her knees. "I'll be back," she told Denise.

Her father's car was idling in the long driveway, headlights turned off. He rolled down the window when Caroline approached but wouldn't shut off the engine and get out until she told him to. When he did, he closed the car door gently.

"Does she know I'm here?"

"Not yet." Caroline resisted the urge to take her father's arm. He was looking around at everything with a blank expression. There was the stable with all the lights glowing inside. How many times had he gone into that barn looking for Joyce, trying to draw her out? There was the lighted path leading the way to the farmhouse, the very house he had picked out with Joyce. *For* Joyce. He never would have lived out here if it weren't for her love of horses.

"Christ," Tom said. "Has it really been eleven years?"

"Sometimes it feels longer."

"I remember this driveway. It was hell when it snowed." He looked to the barn. "I assume she's in there?"

"Yes, with the mare and foal. They're both fine now. You just missed the vet."

Tom walked toward the barn and Caroline hurried ahead so she could show him to the roan's stall. When they got there, Denise was leaning against the wall inside, watching the mother and foal. She turned to Tom calmly, as if she'd been expecting him.

"Hello, Tom," she said. "Meet Diamond." The foal skittered around on his long skinny legs. Denise glanced at Caroline. "I think that's what I'll call him," she said. "On account of his markings. Plus it makes me think of Neil, which makes me think of your mother." The foal did have a crooked, diamond-shaped star on his forehead.

Tom watched the roan rub her muzzle against Diamond's back as the colt started to nurse. "You took care of her," he said. He sounded surprised.

Denise pushed her hair out of her face. She looked dirty and ragged but happy. "These two will be fine on their own for a little while. You want some coffee, Tom?"

It was late, so late it was now early, but he said yes. Denise left the stall, bolting it shut behind her, and led them out of the barn and toward the farm house. Caroline started to follow but drifted back before they reached the front door.

"I want to check on them one more time," she said. "Save me some coffee."

Denise waved her off and led Tom into the house. Caroline paused outside, straining to hear the sound of their voices flickering through the open windows. Denise was giving Tom a tour, showing him what changes she and Joyce made to the house over the years. He didn't seem to be saying much of anything, or if he was, his voice was too low for Caroline to make out.

Caroline went back into the stable and entered the roan's stall again. By now, mother and foal looked a bit cross to have a human intruding in their space yet again. Caroline picked out the rest of the soiled bedding and brought in clean straw. She piled extra straw in the corner and sat down on it. The barn was quiet. The roan dozed on her feet. Caroline closed her eyes, too.

When she woke, it was daybreak. She left the stall with the intent to return to the house and fall right into bed, but first she took one pass down the barn aisle. Birds were coming to life in the rafters and in the trees outside. A barn cat darted into the stable with something furry in its mouth and disappeared behind the grain bins.

Caroline stopped at Venus' stall, where the mare faced her with tired eyes. They spent a quiet moment staring at each other.

"Fine," Caroline said. "Fine."

She walked to the tack room and found Venus's bridle, leaving the saddle behind. Venus accepted the bit easily and even lowered her head so Caroline could pull the headpiece over her ears. Joyce's training had paid off.

Caroline led Venus outside. Her father's car was still there. She used a stump as a mounting block and, once on, took a moment to adjust her weight over Venus' back. The mare was just as she had imagined: solid, strong, warm. The braided leather reins felt slick and recently oiled in Caroline's hands. She wondered if she could still ride the way she used to. It had been so long.

She urged Venus toward the pastures, where they could ride out in the open toward the still-rising sun. Caroline maneuvered Venus carefully so she could reach down to unlatch the gate, but Venus did not spook. She waited patiently, pricking her ears toward the new day.

They entered the pasture and Caroline urged Venus into a trot up the hill. Venus tried to break into a canter, but Caroline held her back. Several horses in adjacent pastures caught sight of them and ran along their own fence lines to follow, their tails streaming through the air. At the top of the hill, Caroline slowed Venus to a walk so they could descend in careful, measured steps. Venus felt steady and sure. The wind picked up, and Caroline gripped the mare's sides a bit tighter, preparing for Venus to bolt, but nothing happened.

They rode next to the ditch at the bottom of the hill, where Caroline pulled Venus to a halt. Caroline closed her eyes and took a breath. She couldn't see the other horses, but they were there. She could smell them, that rich dirt and horsehair smell, warm straw and loose sawdust, the soft whiskery brush of their muzzles. They were always there, somewhere in the corner of her mind, in the place that links smell to memory.

Even without Joyce, and even with her uncertainties about country life, Denise was going to stay on at the farm. She had told Caroline this last night, sometime after Diamond had started nursing for the first time. She would rent out space to a new trainer. With the help of the stable hands, she would raise the roan's foal, turning him into something she thought Joyce would love.

But first, Denise wanted to bury Joyce's ashes somewhere on the property, maybe at the top of one of the hills overlooking the horse fields. Caroline had offered to help. She could already see the two of them kneeling on the grass, placing the urn in the earth and breathing in the smell of dirt, of wind, of horses.

Caroline swung down to the ground and reached up to unbuckle the bridle and slide it off. Venus shook her head, freed within a fenced pasture, and looked toward the other horses in the distance. The wind kicked up again, and Venus spun around and took off at a canter, her hooves pounding out a three-beat rhythm.

As Caroline made her way back to the barn, she saw Denise and her father exit the house. They walked next to each other, tilting their heads together in conversation. She slid under the fence rails and joined them.

"Look at that." Tom pointed. Venus was making another lap around the pasture, her canter lengthening into a gallop as she thundered past them. She crested the hill and disappeared down the other side. "I remember when she was just a baby," he said. "Look at her now."

They waited for Venus to reappear, to gallop past yet again. She never did. She stayed in the far side of the pasture, where Joyce had fallen. With that wide grassy field stretching into the horizon, it was easy to imagine she had never been there at all.

The fall was an accident, Caroline told herself as she scanned the pasture. An accident that could no more be prevented than the roan giving birth, or spring becoming summer.

"I'm glad I came," Tom said. "Though I can't say I'll ever be back."

"This place isn't for everyone," Denise told him.

"It's not for you, either." He looked at Denise. "We both came here for Joyce. Once that connection is cut, that's it."

"I'm not sure about that," Caroline said. She took a long look at the stable, the outdoor arena, the jumps set up and waiting. "There's something here that doesn't end. It goes on and on."

Caroline wished she could tell them about Caroline Kennedy riding that pony across the White House lawn. She was convinced that her namesake was still there, if only in memory or in old issues of *Life* magazine, trotting Macaroni over the manicured grass. In that same way, Caroline saw herself on Cimarron in these fields.

She saw her mother with Venus. If she thought far enough ahead, she saw Denise leading Diamond down the driveway, teaching him to walk on the halter and lead line. He would long to be wild, running up and down the hillsides, but he would stay next to her. With every step by her side he would forgive her hold on him and gradually, with caution, learn to trust.

Laura Maylene Walter has received Ohioana Library Association's Walter Rumsey Marvin grant and Washington College's Sophie Kerr Prize, the nation's largest undergraduate literary award. Her writing has appeared in *Poets & Writers*, *The Writer*, *American Literary Review*, *Inkwell*, and elsewhere, and her novel-in-progress has been a James Jones First Novel Fellowship finalist. She grew up in Lancaster, Pennsylvania, and has resided in the Cleveland area since 2004. She works as an editor of a trade magazine and lives with her husband and their two cats in Lakewood, Ohio. She discusses truth, fiction, and the writing life at lauramaylenewalter.com.

An Interview with Laura Maylene Walter

by Nicholas Sawin

Q. Congratulations on your selection for the G.S. Sharat Chandra Prize for Short Fiction. What themes do you see under the umbrella of your new book's title: Living Arrangements? *How do you see these stories forming a cohesive collection?*

A. I'm thrilled to be the Chandra Prize winner and have my debut collection published by BkMk Press, so thank you.

I wrote the stories in *Living Arrangements* over a period of about five years. At the time, I didn't realize I was building a collection— I was just writing short stories. But of course certain themes emerged, and I eventually saw that I might have a collection on my hands.

I have always considered the story "Living Arrangements" to be the heart of this collection. It introduces the theme of searching for a place in the world and feeling that something vital has been left in the past. Just as the narrator in the title story returns to visit her former homes, the other characters in the collection are determining where they belong and, often, reconciling the past as they move forward.

Q. In the title story, your protagonist's whole life unfolds through the succession of homes she occupies. Do you consider place, particularly the home, to reflect the characters within? What inspiration do you derive from place in your stories? As an unapologetic coffee shop writer, does your sense of your own place have an effect on your work?

A. I grew up in Lancaster, PA, and still feel a strong connection to the landscapes there—the rolling hills, the valleys, the farmland, the rural back roads. I haven't lived there for years, and every time I go back I feel simultaneously linked to my hometown and also distanced from it. I can never return to how it was for me to grow up there, but sometimes I wish I could. Some of the characters in this collection feel the same way, including the narrator in the title story, who has left parts of herself behind in her former homes.

And yes, "unapologetic coffee shop writer" is a good way to describe me. As recently as several years ago, I couldn't imagine doing the majority of my writing in public. I have since found, however, that removing myself from the distractions of home and physically relocating to a different place can jumpstart my writing sessions. My ideal place to write would be a private cabin in the woods somewhere, but since that's not a possibility right now, the local café will have to do the trick.

Q. *Your short stories often feature thorny or even toxic mother-daughter relationships such as Shelly and her mother in "The Clarinet," Tabitha and Gladys in "A System Based on Counting," and Caroline and Joyce in "Return to Stillbrook Farm." While in other interviews you have made a distinction between your characters and your own biography, how do you walk that line between personal revelation and fictional reimagining in your work? How has your own mother's death from cancer influenced your fiction?*

A. I was 20 years old when my mother died, rather suddenly, from cancer. For several years after her death, I wrote about grief and death and mothers and daughters. While I've mostly moved past those themes, they continue to occasionally emerge in my writing in one form or another.

It's true that some stories in *Living Arrangements*, as well as my current novel in progress, feature strained or toxic mother-daughter relationships. Here I need to point out that my mom wasn't anything like my fictional mothers— she and I were very close and had a positive relationship. I think these themes in my fiction reveal my continued exploration of loss and severed mother-daughter relationships. Only in these cases, the divide is caused by conflict instead of death.

As is the case with many writers, my fiction may sometimes contain autobiographical elements, but I branch out and make things up until I can barely recognize the story's original catalyst. For example, I played the clarinet as a child, just like the narrator in "The Clarinet," and I rode horses like Caroline in "Return to Stillbrook

Farm." (Sadly, I was not nearly as talented or as accomplished at these activities as my characters.) But that is largely where the similarities end—the events take on a new life for me on the page.

Q. In "To Elizabeth Bishop, with Love," an unnamed narrator pens a letter to the deceased poet and short story writer, offering a gloomy take on the fate of literature in the modern world of technology and media obsession. Do you share her concerns, as an author and a blogger?

A. I suppose I do, though I'd like to point out that the narrator's circumstances—both as a middle school teacher and as someone suffering from a health crisis—prompt her to be more negative about these things than I would be. I do worry, however, that the simple act of sitting down and quietly reading for several hours is becoming an increasingly rare practice, particularly among young people, and that does concern me.

On the other hand, what do I know? I'm not a teacher or librarian and I also can't discount the recent surge in the popularity of YA novels. But yes, it's something that has crossed my mind.

Q. In this collection, women explore and broaden objectified roles, such as a lingerie model in a shop window ("Live Model") and a figure skater performing before a stalker ("The Ballad Solemn of Lady Malena"). What interests you about examining the superficiality or the beauty of women on display?

A. These are issues that most young girls face as they grow up, even if on a subconscious level, as they internalize the fact that they are on display in the world as sexual beings. How does this impact a girl or young woman's gathering understanding of herself and her place in the world? How does she rise above, or at least confront, these realities? Those were questions I had in mind while writing these particular stories.

The young woman in "Live Model" has spent her entire life being judged—in a negative light—solely for her unusual physical appearance; she only begins to receive some semi-positive attention when she models lingerie. Yet she has a lively sense of humor and rich inner life. Similarly, Annabelle in "The Ballad Solemn of Lady Malena," who is growing up in the strict confines of the elite figure skating world, tries for the first time to claim some control over her circumstances. I wanted to give these young women their own voices and a more complete picture of who they are aside from their perceived sex appeal (or lack thereof).

Q. *How do you balance being a writer, wife, cat owner, journalist, trade magazine editor, and blogger (at LauraMayleneWalter.com)? Do you find that these roles bleed into each other? Does your role as a fiction writer shape your voice as an essayist or journalist, and vice-versa? Are there advantages to moving between these genres?*

A. Balance is the key word. I'm the type of person who always tries to do everything at once, to add yet another activity or deadline to my plate, but sometimes that just isn't possible. I've had to learn the art of focusing on one thing and letting certain others go—at least for the moment.

I've worked as an editor of a trade magazine for the last four years, and despite the fact that it consumes a lot of mental energy, it's had a positive impact on my creative work. I'm a perfectionist, which means I'm inclined to agonize over a piece of writing forever, second-guess myself, and wait as long as possible before showing it to someone else (writing groups excluded—I have no shame when it comes to submitting work to be critiqued). As anyone in journalism knows, this kind of hesitancy just isn't possible while writing on deadline.

My job has helped me learn to write faster, edit faster, pull pieces together faster, and then get it out there and get on with it. Fiction demands a different type of creative process, of course, but my day job has strengthened my ability to simply sit down and get to work. Similarly, my personal blog has improved some aspects of both my professional work and my fiction—it's just more writing practice and another way to learn how to organize my thoughts, write honestly, and let my voice emerge. The blog might be time consuming, but I'm not convinced my fiction has suffered for it. I steal the time I use to blog from other activities.

I'm fortunate to have a husband who is supportive of my writing; I can't even imagine him complaining about the hours I spend holed up in cafés with my laptop. Finally, while I like to joke about being a cat lady, my cats don't add much to my busy schedule—except when they interrupt my writing or reading to demand attention, which, frankly, they probably deserve.

Q. How have your literary tastes changed over the years? What writers have influenced or inspired your work? Which authors do you consider to be kindred spirits? Do you consider yourself to be writing from a certain tradition?

A. I love Ann Patchett and Margaret Atwood. Books like *Evening* by Susan Minot, *Anywhere But Here* by Mona Simpson, *The History of Love* by Nicole Krauss, *Unless* by Carol Shields, and *Olive Kitteridge* by Elizabeth Strout are also inspirations. I love the magic in Aimee Bender's fiction, and I try to keep that sort of playfulness in mind while writing pieces like "Live Model."

Q. What's next for you? With the publication of your first book, what writerly goals have you set for yourself?

A. I've been working on a novel for the past few years. The manuscript has received some recognition in the form of an Ohioana grant and a fellowship runner-up designation, but I still can't say how close the novel is to being finished. It's a slow, evolutionary process.

In addition to the novel, I'm working on more short stories— I've been flooded with new ideas these days—as well as some personal essays. My goal is to eventually publish a novel and a second short story collection. But to quote Isak Dinesen, I'm ultimate trying to write "without hope and without despair."

Discussion Questions

1. In the book's title story, Walter encapsulates a woman's life through her physical connection to the various homes where she has lived. What connection does this story reveal between place and the progression of this woman's life? How do the brief sketches of each home create a sense of that life? What trajectory do you believe the story would take if it continued beyond these pages? Would the absent mother return? Which places from your own past would you haunt if given the chance?

2. How does the lingerie model in "Live Model" challenge conventional ideas about beauty? Do you think the story says something about the cult of celebrity and women's bodies on display? How does the final scene contrast with the modeling described in the rest of the story?

3. In the story "The Clarinet," does the clarinet itself represent something more? What role does perfectionism play in the disintegration of this toxic mother-daughter relationship? Have you ever experienced the same sense of "flow" as the narrator's performance before her classmates? What does the ending suggest to you about young girls' differing paths toward coming of age?

4. Were you surprised by the point of view of the stalker of a teenage figure skater in "The Ballad Solemn of Lady Malena"? How did the story's point of view affect your feelings for the characters? How do you think the story plays with the roles of audience/performer, adult/child, man/woman?

5. In "To Elizabeth Bishop, with Love," the narrator writes a letter to Bishop honoring the surprising similarities between herself and a famous poet. If you could pen such a letter, to whom would you write it, and for what would you thank him or her? How does the narrator deal with the futility of writing a letter to someone who will never receive it?

6. What do the stories in *Living Arrangements* say about being a fan, an admirer, an observer of life? Are such characters in some way outsiders in life? Do these stories view a new generation of women as outsiders?

7. How does the character Ariel in "The Last Halloween" connect with Sylvia Plath's poetry book of the same name? How does the maturity of Plath's literature match or contrast with the narrator's own coming of age on Halloween night? In what ways does this story look at realistic fear versus make-believe fear for children? What qualities make Ariel a complicated character?

8. In "How to Speak Czech," how does Alema discover her heritage through her grandmother? Is Alema's story in any way a larger American story? What lasting effects have America's melting pot culture had on Alema? On you?

9. In "Return to Stillbrook Farm," daughter Caroline reexamines her connections to a horse-training farm after her mother's accidental death. How does this place attract and repel her at the same time? Could the horses stand in for any larger thematic issues in the story?

Previous winners of the
G.S. Sharat Chandra Prize for Short Fiction

A Bed of Nails by Ron Tanner
selected by Janet Burroway

I'll Never Leave You by H. E. Francis
selected by Diane Glancy

The Logic of a Rose by Billy Lombardo
selected by Gladys Swan

Necessary Lies by Kerry Neville Bakken
selected by Hilary Masters

Love Letters from a Fat Man by Naomi Benaron
selected by Stuart Dybek

Tea and Other Ayama Na Tales by Eleanor Bluestein
selected by Marly Swick

Dangerous Places by Perry Glasser
selected by Gary Gildner

Georgic by Mariko Nagai
selected by Jonis Agee